T0086351

TASTE THE WIND

TASTE THE WIND

Robert Livingston

TASTE THE WIND

iUniverse books may be ordered through booksellers or by contacting:

iUniverse
1663 Liberty Drive
Bloomington, IN 47403
www.iuniverse.com
844-349-9409

ISBN: 978-1-6632-2263-3 (sc)
ISBN: 978-1-6632-2264-0 (e)

Print information available on the last page.

iUniverse rev. date: 05/19/2021

CONTENTS

PART III
The Boys of Crescent City

PART IV
Destiny

DEDICATION

To my father, Samuel Livingston, who served in the U.S. Navy in both World War I and II, and who also "tasted the wind" in the Civilian Conservation Corps, 1933-1935. Thanks for your service and for keeping the family together during difficult times.

Your son, Robert

A FEW WORDS

Samuel Livingston was my father. Initially, I intended to write a story about my father's experiences in the C.C.C. --- the Civilian Conservation Corps, which was established by Congress in 1933 at the urging of President Franklin D. Roosevelt (FDR). In doing so, I was going to focus on a forest fire my father wrote about in 1934 for a C.C.C. publication called *Youth Rebuilds.* In time I shifted the focus. I set for myself the challenge of expanding his dramatic, very romanticized short story with a present day account of an out-of-control fire raging along the Oregon-California border.

Almost immediately, I was faced with the question of what would start my fictionalized fire? Arson, always a good possibility, held no interest for me, nor did city folks leaving their campfire unattended, or a car backfiring. These causes seemed so pedestrian. A lightning strike, while believable, seemed to lack punch, even if it crackled with danger. Some unsupervised children playing with matches were always an option but not one I liked. College students smoking pot in the great outdoors had a limited appeal. No, I needed something that titillated both the reader and my interest.

In time a thought drifted across my mind and through the skies above. What if a balloon started my forest fire? Not just any balloon, of course, but a Japanese World War II balloon bomb. According to military historians, over 9,000 of such balloons were released by the Japanese Imperial Army in late 1944 and through the first months of 1945. During a four to five day period, these lethal balloons floated across the Pacific high up in the jet stream. Eventually, many of them reached the West Coast where some detonated in the forests of Washington State and Oregon. This led to many questions. What if one balloon didn't explode? What if years later something caused it to do so? What if the result was a terrifying forest fire?

Of course, if I were writing about a low tech Japanese effort to create the world's first intercontinental weapon, how would I connect that history to my father's C.C.C. experiences a decade before the balloon bomb campaign? Again, I was rescued by a thought not initially on my mind's sketch board. Why not have a fictitious young man, Matt Samuels, interview his grandfather (my real dad) about a topic for his high school history class? The setting would be a VA Hospital in San Francisco. In this encounter the history of the C.C.C. would be reborn, even as the life of one former enlistee in "Roosevelt's Tree Army" ebbed.

Other ideas rushed in, each clamoring for typing space, as I thought through the plotline. Would it be possible for Matt to be a latter day hero by actually fighting a contemporary forest fire in 1966? Well, of course, it would be. The writer is in charge, isn't he? In my vision Matt would be a summer worker with the California State Division of Forestry (C.D.F.), and through that fictional experience, he would relive my own five summers with the same outfit while attending college. In the end he would face a life and death situation caused by a balloon bomb, which by chance, fate, or a higher plan finally detonated.

The story is presented in three parts. Part I will focus on the Japanese balloon bombs. Part II will center on the C.C.C. Part III will emphasize the C.D.F. Always, fire in its many manifestations, either as a wartime instrument of the military, or a naturally occurring phenomenon, will be the backdrop of this narrative and what connected all to "taste the wind."

Enjoy.

Robert Livingston,
2021

FIRE QUOTATIONS

Man is the only creature that dares to light a fire and live with it. The reason? Because he alone has learned to put it out.

Henry Jackson Vandyke, Jr.

Fire, water and government know nothing of mercy.

Proverbs

Fires all go out eventually.

Unknown

Part I

PRELUDE

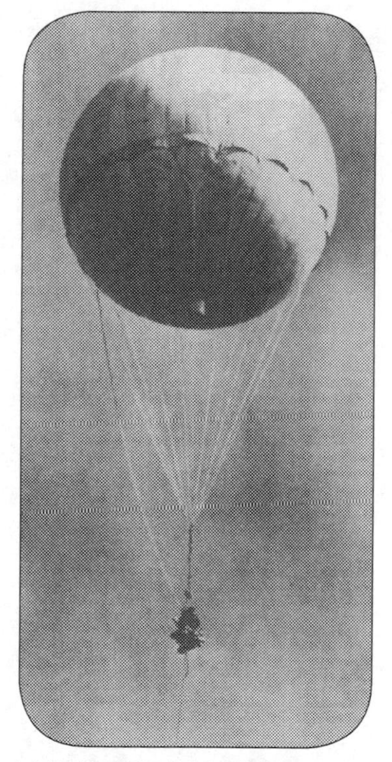

A JAPANESE BALLOON BOMB

Chapter 1

ANTICIPATING WAR

FEBRUARY 1941 – THE WHITE HOUSE

The storm was coming, and seemingly, nothing could stop it. Already the morning skies above the capitol had grown increasingly dark and ominous, as if some malevolent spirit was animating the armada of ghost-like clouds, which hung over the city. To the east, out in the cold Atlantic, the storm was born in the incubator of a vast low-pressure area approximately 200-miles off the coast. As the storm grew in size and intensity, it charged westward, blowing past tired fishing boats and bulky freighters, and an occasional cruise ship, leaving all careening in troubled waters. Near the coast, a few frigate birds whipped their wings in the increasing high winds in mute testimony to the gale forces descending on the approaching shoreline, where once the storm made landfall, the rains would begin.

The storm had come to Washington D.C.

That morning several vehicles meandered through the wet city streets bearing important personages to the White House. Two of the vehicles, late model Ford sedans, came from Alexandria on the Virginia side of the Potomac River. As they did, its passengers could view the somber

Washington Monument and the magnificent Jefferson Memorial this cold and dreary morning. An older model Plymouth carried another passenger from Silver Springs, Maryland just east of Rock Creek Park and not far from Walter Reed Hospital. A spritely painted dark blue Buick with its heavy metal grille grinning-humanlike purred its way past the Lincoln Memorial. Its passenger wondered if the great man knew what was brewing in the wind. The last people attending the White House this day took Yellow Cabs from trendy Georgetown and the less trendy Stanton Park area.

Oblivious to what was transpiring below, the great storm drenched the city in a torrent of cold rain accompanied by booming claps of thunder and jagged lightning flashing through the early morning skies. Through this maelstrom, the cars moved uneasily toward their impromptu, unscheduled meeting.

White House guards, both civilian and military, bearing large, black umbrellas to care for the visitors, carefully checked these officials, though they were exceedingly well known to everyone. They were members of the President Franklin D. Roosevelt's cabinet. They were constantly in the public's eye, and according to their critics, even in the public's face. The guards noticed that their visitors were grim-faced on this Sunday morning, February 7, 1941. The guards could read the tea leaves as well as anyone. Something was up.

The individuals in question were quickly ushered into the East Wing and then hurriedly escorted to the Oval Office, where their boss waited for them with poorly disguised impatience. When they were finally assembled, the "old man" got right down to business.

The Office of President Franklin D. Roosevelt

"Perhaps it's too early for something stronger than coffee," the President said with a twinkle in his eye, "but a little brandy just might help given our rather painful agenda today. Anyone?"

No one asked for brandy.

Trying to break the tension in the room, Harry Hopkins, the chain-smoking aide to the President, said, "Fortunately, the brandy is legal now that "prohibition" is history. Any takers?"

Again, there were no takers. Instead, black coffee was poured to take the chill off this wet morning.

Maneuvering his wheelchair in front of the famous Resolute desk, so named because it was built from the timbers of the British frigate *HMS Resolute*, and was given to the United States as a present by Queen Victoria in 1880, the President said, "Cordell, bring us up to date."

"Mr. President, the situation is increasingly dreadful and highly dangerous. We are, I'm afraid, on a path which will lead to war with the Empire of Japan."

Those in the room were no longer startled by this prediction. They had heard it more often in recent days. The Far East was aflame.

As Secretary of State since 1933, Secretary of State Cordell Hull had increasingly focused in on this prophecy since New Year's Day. Born in a log cabin in Pickett County, Tennessee in 1871, the "Judge," as he was known, was not a man to mix words. Twenty-four years in the House of Representatives had taught him the ways of Washington, and the need for clarity when important issues were discussed. He had proved this to himself as the author of the first Federal Income Tax bill during President Woodrow Wilson's administration. It had been reinforced by his efforts to lower trade tariffs with other countries, and his promotion of the President's Good Neighbor Policy in the Western Hemisphere.

"We already know what's happening in China. We know what took place in Korea and Manchuria. Japan has been at war in Asia since 1931. We've condemned her policies of aggression."

"As we should," said the Secretary of War, Henry I. Stimson, the only nominal member of the Republican Party in the President's cabinet. "The

Japanese mean to expand their empire by any means, certainly by force if necessary."

"I agree," Hull said sadly.

"What will be their next move?" the President asked.

"Aggressive moves in Southeast Asia and especially the big prize, the Philippines," Stimson said. "And that would mean war with the United States."

"They wouldn't," said Frances Perkins, the only woman in the room."

"I'm afraid Henry is right, Madam Secretary of Labor," Hull added.

"And that flaunts our policy, the Stimson Doctrine, am I not correct?" asked Hopkins.

"It does," Stimson said flatly. ""We have told the Japanese the United States would not recognize any changes made in violation of existing treaties. That has been and continues to be our official policy."

"Tokyo's response?" asked Hopkins.

"As expected, they refuse to acknowledge the policy. The Japanese government, led by the military, I might add, refuses to yield to what they consider to be unwarranted international diplomatic pressure."

"George, you've been unusually silent. "What are your thoughts?"

General of the Armies, George Catlett Marshall had a long and impressive career in the U.S. military. A graduate of the Virginia Military Institute, he had served in the Philippines after the Spanish-American War. He was an aide to General John Pershing during the Great War. Later he was the Assistant Commander of the army's infantry school. He carried with him a quiet dignity and an intense desire to rebuild the American military.

"As things are now," Marshall said, "we will be at war within a year. And we will go into it ill-prepared to fight both Germany and Japan, the Axis partners."

The Oval Office, first designed and built during the administration of William Howard Taft in 1906, was quiet. The thought of war hung heavily in the room. The President broke the silence.

"As usual, George, your point is unfortunately not only direct, but true. We are playing catch up with Tokyo and Berlin. And time, I'm afraid, is running out. Which brings me to the subject of this meeting. A decision must be made. A very expensive decision, as you know. We need to talk about the 'special project.' I read over the report you provided George. As always, you stated the case quite clearly, as you did for after the necessary appropriation. Am I correct" the President asked, "that the cost will be $3-billion for this plane?"

"If the project is fully funded and over 4,000 planes are built, yes that is the predicted cost."

"We're talking nine zeroes," the President added caustically. "That's more than the other project," he said.

Known only to a few people, the proposed other super secret appropriation was for the Manhattan Project. The cost for splitting the atom and building the ultimate bomb was projected to be $2.5-billion.

"Please recall," Marshall hastily added, "after considerable debate, the last Congress reluctantly provided the initial funding for the plane in 1939 to replace the older B17 bomber."

But the cost," the President exclaimed. "These new projections..."

"Perhaps I can explain," interrupted the Air Force's top officer, Hap Arnold.

"General."

"We are contracting with the Boeing Company to build a super-fortress, the largest bomber ever constructed on a mass scale. We call it the B-29. If we go to war we will need a plane that can carry the war to Japan, assuming we have bases in the Pacific from which to launch attacks. Nothing like this plane has ever been built before. It will be bigger and faster than anything in the air."

"To build 4,000 planes, we will need over 50,000 workers and 3,000 or more sub-contractors," Marshall added.

"The B-29," Arnold pointed out, "will have a range in excess of 5,000 miles. It will fly above 30,000 feet at a speed of 370 m.p.h. The Wright Corporation in Kansas will build the plane's four engines. Each engine will generate 2200 horsepower making it the most powerful propeller-driven bomber in the world. The Boeing Company has designed a state of the art plane."

"And an exceedingly expensive one," the President again reminded his guests."

"This plane is designed for high-altitude strategic bombings, but will also excel in low-altitude night bombing using incendiary bombing," Hap Arnold interjected. "And unlike the B-17, this plane will be pressurized and all the guns will be remote-controlled. It will also have an extraordinary high payload."

"It will carry 20,000 pounds of high explosives, Marshall confided. If necessary, this plane will bring the war to Japan proper."

The President listened to his two generals for whom he had immense respect. Though he had already made up his mind to fund the project, still he was still disturbed by its cost.

"How will Boeing be paid?" the President asked.

"The anticipated contract called for a "cost-plus fixed fee." Stimson said. "The government will pay for all legitimate costs and provide Boeing with a 6% profit. The same formula will be used with all sub-contractors."

"Frances," the President said, "would you like to comment?"

The President had known Frances Perkins for a long time. When he was Governor of New York, she had served as the state industrial commissioner, where she sought to improve the working conditions of women, establish a minimum wage for all workers, and define a maximum workweek. Beyond that, she battled for a program of unemployment compensation. When the President moved from Albany to Washington D.C., he appointed her Secretary of Labor, making her the first woman to hold a U.S. cabinet post

"As a woman, I realize men will be men. If they are intent upon war, there will be war. As the Secretary of Labor, I see this B-29 contract as an immense work project, which should employ many thousands of people."

The President smiled to himself. That's my Frances. Tell it likes she sees it. Behind the scenes, he knew, she had drafted the legislation, which became the Social Security Act of 1935 and the Fair Labor Standards Act of 1938. She was a fighter for improving the working conditions across America. She also worked hard at stimulating employment. Frances, he reminded himself, had not endeared herself to conservative Republicans, who saw her reforms as detrimental to the free market. But then again, he hadn't either. For many, he was now the political anti-Christ destroying unfettered capitalism.

"If I may, Mr. President," Perkins said, "I'd like to double check a few items with the generals."

"Of course."

"According to the report, I was given," she said, there will be war plants in Tacoma, Everett, Bellingham, all in Washington state where Boeing is located."

"That is correct," Marshall said. "But there will also be production facilities in Wichita, Kansas and Marietta, Georgia. In fact, the plant #6 in Marietta will be the largest aircraft assembly installation in the world."

"And in Seattle," Stimson added, "there the world's largest wind tunnel will be constructed at a cost approaching $1,000,000."

"Why all the questions?" Hap Arnold asked. "To build this bomber will cost a ton of money. We all know that."

"What we don't know," Perkins said almost angrily is how the workers will be treated, their pay and, especially in the South? How Negroes will be treated with respect to employment opportunities. The same goes for women."

There she goes thought the President, right to the heart of the matter, at least for her.

"If we go to war," Stimson said," we will have over 10,000,000 men and women in the armed forces. Perhaps even more. All other adults and even teenagers will find jobs in the defense industries. We will need all our citizens, regardless of gender or race."

"If we go to war," Hopkins said quietly.

The President ended the discussion, saying, "The funding will be provided. Congress will do so reluctantly... I have only one question," he continued, "I know how we intend to bomb Japan with the B-29 if it comes to that, but how will the Japanese, if they decide on war, attack us?"

"That is the question," Stimson said.

Ten months later on December 7, 1941 the question was answered at a relatively unknown American naval bastion in the Pacific --- Pearl Harbor.

THE B-29 SUPRFORTRESS

Chapter 2

FUSEN BAKUDAN

SEPTEMBER – 1941 – NORTHERN JAPAN

The most northern Japanese province is Hokkaido (See Map, Page 16). On the tortuous and rugged east coast where the weather storms in from the North Pacific Ocean is the small fishing village of Kushiro, whose people have harvested the water's bounty for ages. Also, located here in 1941 was a cluster of wooden buildings, which were fenced off from the town's inhabitants in order to maintain secrecy. This was the headquarters of the Imperial Japanese Army's technical research center. Here basic research was conducted to develop either new weapons or to improve on existing ones.

In September of 1941, the center was focused on an exotic, low-tech weapon designed to advantage the Japanese military in case war ensued in the Pacific basin with the United States. Paradoxically, the current research was focused on the cutting edge of the past and a particularity of nature.

In the private office of the Commanding Officer two men were enjoying a cup of tea and rice cakes. In the quiet of the morning they were also discussing Japan's future.

One of the two men, Major General Sueyoshi Kusaba, was older and a veteran of many military campaigns. He was in his late 50's, a stocky and strong man, who had survived the Russo-Japanese War of 1905 and Japan's more recent incursions in China. He was the director of the research complex, a position given to him due to his engineering background and the severe wounds he suffered near Nanking. The Chinese nationalists had not, as he had been led to believe, simply rolled over before the advancing Imperial Japanese Army. Now, not quite retired, yet far from the scene of action, he was restive, a man of action landlocked by his Tokyo superiors.

He was a unique individual in many respects. Raised in Japan near Kyoto, the traditional religious capital of the nation, he was a firm believer in the Shinto philosophy and an uncontested worship of the Emperor. But he was also a man who had traveled widely, including four years in the United States when he attended the University of Wisconsin, and from where he graduated with an advanced degree in engineering. His friends and colleagues knew him as a thoughtful person and a devoted reader of historical biographies, especially those touching upon military history and curiously, the America Civil War. He considered himself somewhat an authority on both Generals U.S. Grant and Robert E. Lee.

Seated across from him was his "make it happen guy," Major Teiji Takada, a young engineering graduate from Yokohama. Recognized as an excellent university student, who was keen on basic research, he was spared the Chinese wars. Unlike Kusaba, he had not traveled much beyond the four main Japanese islands, which composed the country. Born in a suburb of Tokyo, he had a limited understanding of the outside world. Again, rather than being sent to the "killing grounds" of China, he was assigned to the technical center to design and test new weapons. His boss, Kusaba, had taken an immediate liking to him, particularly because of the young man's clear analytical mind, which focused dead hard on problem solving.

In some ways, Kusaba treated Takada like a son. Perhaps this was because two sons had died in China. To some extent the professional companionship provided by the young engineer ameliorated that loss. Unexpectedly, the Commander also treated the young man as a confidant.

Sensing the Future

On this day, September 7, 1`941, Kusaba waxed philosophically about Japan's destiny.

"Teiji, what are we going to do?"
"Sir?"
"We are preparing for a war we cannot win."
"I don't understand."

Teiji was more than surprised to hear his superior speak in this manner. There seemed to be in Kursaba's voice some inevitable and dreadful understanding of the future

"We will soon be at war with the Americans."
"If so, we will win, Major General."
"The first year and perhaps a little more, the Pacific will be under our flag, but then ..."
"The Americans are soft. They will not fight."
"Teiji, do not believe everything Tokyo tells you. I've been to America and I have studied her history, especially their Civil War. The country has immense production facilities and a raw frontier fighting spirit. If Japan makes war on these people, they will fight."
"You've shared your opinions with the Combined Chiefs?"
"Yes."
"And?"
"They believe their own propaganda, Teiji. Ever since 1905, they've happily and foolishly convinced themselves in the supremacy of the Japanese warrior and nation."

The younger man understood the Major General was referring to the Russo-Japanese War for control of the Korean peninsula, Manchuria, and Russia's Far East outposts, most importantly, Port Arthur.

"You remember, Teiji, how that war began?"
"Only from the history books," he said with a smile. "Admiral Togo attacked at night, February 8,1905, when the Czar's fleet was asleep."

"Without a declaration of war..."

"It was surprise attack, Sir, a glorious victory against the Europeans."

"It was, " the older man said almost despondently.

"Sir, why are your spirits so downcast?"

"I fear the Imperial Navy will do it again, this time against the Americans."

"And we will win as before."

"The Americans, Teiji, are not the Russians. They have a great fleet."

"We will destroy it."

"Perhaps, Teiji, if the Americans have a Port Arthur."

"They do."

"Oh?"

"Pearl Harbor."

The junior officer's words hung in the air. Each man was acquainted with America's naval fortress in Hawaii. Japanese war games had focused for years on this unsinkable aircraft carrier in the Eastern Pacific. How could it be attacked? How to neutralize the American Pacific fleet? Always, the answers lay with a historical precedent. Was there another Admiral Togo, who would prove victorious in a second "battle of Tsushima Straits?"

"Teiji, you are indeed a bright young man. You are very insightful. I'm glad you're with me. Now let's talk about another situation. In the event of war, we must be able to carry the conflict to the United States itself. How can we do this? That is the question before us. Hawaii itself is over 2500 miles from Japan, and the West Coast of America is another 2,000 miles. How do we overcome these distances? We have no plane on the drawing boards, which can fly that far. Unless we actually overrun and occupy the Hawaiian Islands, we cannot launch a fleet attack against the West Coast. Submarine assaults would be limited to a few blasts at shoreline targets. So I ask you again, Teiji, how do we reach the Americans on their home ground?"

The young Major considered what he had heard. The General's words saddened and challenged him. The warrior in him wanted to avoid flinching before the problem. The engineer in him sought to overcome the immutable numbers staring starkly in his face, time and distance, two almost metaphysical fortresses, which might consume all invaders.

"Fusen Bakudan, Sir. That is the answer."

The Major General was fully acquainted with Teiji's answer. He had read Lt. Commander Kiyoshi Tanaka's report months earlier and indeed his own research center was working on turning theory into practice.

REPORT

The "fusen bakudan" or balloon bombs could be assembled and launched from submarines off the American coast. However, many more balloons could and should be launched from our home island, or Japanese controlled islands in the Eastern Pacific. The Fu-go (the Japanese term for fusen barundan or fire bomb) would be a high altitude weapon functioning above 30,000 feet in the jet stream. Hydrogen would be needed to fill the balloon bag. Suitable materials would be needed to create the air bags themselves.

The theory behind this rests on the work of the Japanese meteorologist, Wasaburo Oishi, who discovered a "river of fast moving air currents" in the atmosphere at about 23,000 to 35,000 feet above Mt. Fuji in the 1920's. What he had discovered is now known as the "jet stream." Years later Oishi's research was substantiated by the German meteorologist, Heinrich Seilkopf who was the Director at th German Weather Service in Hamburg. That was in 1939. It was Seikof who coined the words "jet stream," from the German word "strahlstromung," which referred to jet flow in mechanical engineering. Inadvertently, Wiley Post, an American pilot and celebrity, discovered the air current phenomenon while testing planes at 20,000 feet and higher. The testing also included the use of pressurized suits to protect pilots at that elevation. This was in 1934.

The following problems have been identified relative to a balloon bomb. First, can an airbag be constructed strong enough to hold the hydrogen for three days, the minimum number of days to transit the Pacific? Second, how do we stabilize the hydrogen in order to keep the balloon from rising or falling due to changes in day and night temperatures? Third, how heavy a payload could be carried? Fourth, how would the payload be activated automatically once over American territory? Fifth, would such a balloon actually travel at least 5,000 miles? Sixth, how would we know if the balloons successfully accomplished their mission?

"Tanaka did excellent work, Teiji."

"Yes and we have shown through our research that all his concerns can be overcome."

"You and your staff have done outstanding work. But …"

"Sir?"

"Teiji, sadly I must tell you our funding has been stopped. This research center is being denied funds to continue balloon bomb experimentation. It appears the Imperial Combined Staff is more concerned about a looming attack on the Americas than our basic scientific research."

"What can we do, Sir?"

"We must await events."

"Events?"

"Something so dramatic and wrenching, which would change Tokyo's mind."

"What would that be?"

"Something that would crack our national sense of invulnerability. It would be something that would threaten the Emperor and our people, something that would cast doubt in our ability to win a protracted war with the Americans. Something that would dash the morale of the Japanese people, and our national pride."

"But what could do all this?" Teiji asked.

"I'm not sure, but whatever it is, it will most probably come from the Americans."

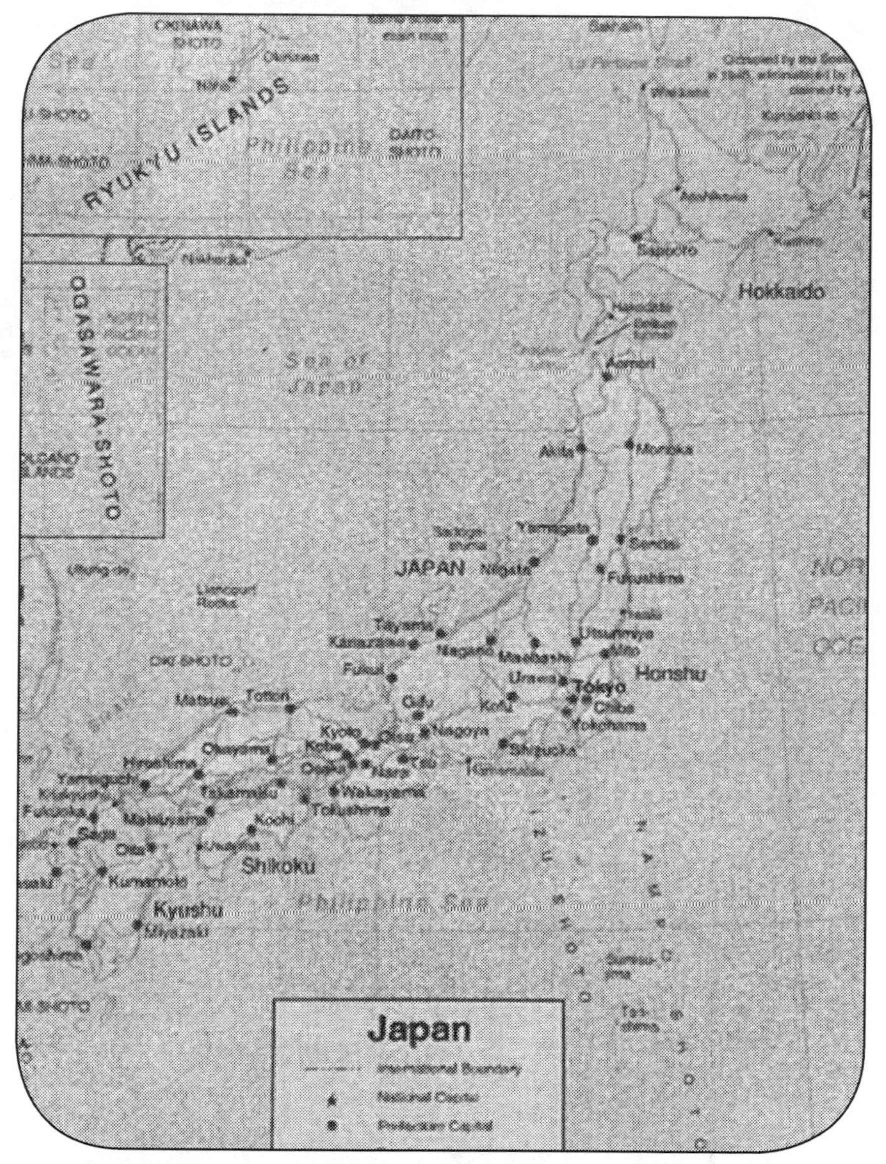

MAP OF JAPAN – HOKKADO – UPPER RIGHT CORNER

Chapter 3

THE HORNET STINGS

APRIL – 1942 – FIGHTING BACK

Americans awoke on April 18, 1942, a shaken people. In just four months since Pearl Harbor, which had been hit in a "surprise attack," the United States had suffered a number of humiliating defeats; the Philippines, Guam, and Wake Island had passed out of American hands. They had seen the British, Dutch, and French vanquished from Southeast Asia, permitting her people, military bases, and raw materials to fall under Japan's purview.

Everywhere, it seemed, Nippon was on the march. Everywhere the United States was on the defensive.

The news was equally bad from Europe, where the Nazis hordes were at the doorsteps of Leningrad, Moscow, and Stalingrad in the greatest land battles in history. England was still reeling from the "blitz" and North Africa was in danger of being overrun by Erwin Rommel's desert legion. At sea, the German "wolf packs" continued to extract a terrible price from Allied shipping. The Atlantic was a graveyard of merchant ships and their precious cargoes.

Everywhere the Axis was grinding away toward victory.

In Japan, the good news was broadcasted to a receptive people, "Nippon Triumphant." The American fleet at Pearl Harbor had been destroyed. The European imperialists were retreating. Their colonial empires were gone, ripped from their hands by the victorious Imperial Navy. Japan had replaced the former colonial powers. Japan's vision of a "Co-prosperity Sphere" was coming true--- that is, Asians for Asians under Tokyo's rule. Only the protracted conflict in China gave less jingoistic people a reason to pause.

On this day there were, however, timid signs of hope in America. The draft had come to the nation big time, and millions of men and women were flooding into the armed forces. A great military force was being raised. Throughout the country, the industrial might of America was being harnessed. Where consumer goods were once produced, now planes, tanks, ships, and guns were being manufactured. The armed forces would have all they need to conduct the business of war. In towns and cities, as well as in the suburbs and on the farms, the spirit of an awakened nation was taking hold. "Remember Pearl Harbor" was a rallying cry to justify righteous vengeance on a distant enemy.

Retaliation

The military aide rushed into the Oval Office with the latest dispatch for the President. His meeting with Secretary Stimson was in this case most happily interrupted.

"Sir, the Hornet has stung this day 18 April 1942."

"Thank you. Please leave us now."

"They've really done it, Mr. President. They're on their way."

"Finally. Perhaps in a few hours we will have something to really cheer about."

"And the country, Sir."

The Central Pacific

On April 2, 1942, Task Force 18, led by the aircraft carrier, the *USS Hornet*, quietly left its homeport of Alameda, California and slipped out to sea. To those watching from the Golden Gate Bridge, the warships passing below were heading westward into unknown but dangerous waters. Two weeks later, on April 16th, Task Force 18 rendezvoused with Task Force 16 just north of Hawaii. The combined naval force was under the command of William F. Halsey, Jr. and consisted of two carriers and a number of fast escort ships, and two very slow oil tankers.

The *USS Enterprise* in Task Force 16 was present to protect the fleet if attacked by Japanese carrier planes. From its carrier deck, fighters would rise into the sky to shoot down incoming enemy planes. The *Hornet's* fighters were stowed below deck, however, and could not be used to fend off any foes. This was done in order to clear the flight deck for the "surprise," which was lashed there.

The President and the Secretary knew all about the "surprise."

The origin of the plan dated back to December 21, 1941, only two weeks after Pearl Harbor. The President had told the Joint Chiefs to find a way to bomb Japan in order to boost American morale. At the time, it seemed like an impossible request. A young naval officer, Captain Francis Low, however, submitted a plan to the Chief of Naval Operations, Ernest King, on January 10, 1942, which turned the impossible into at least the improbable. The plan was stunningly simple and completely insane with a poor chance of success. Nevertheless, the plan was made operational. A tough middle-aged officer, James "Jimmy" Doolittle, was placed in charge of the program.

The plan called for twin-engine army bombers to be successfully launched from a carrier, something that had never been done before. The bomber in question would be the B-25B Mitchell, which had a range of possibly 2,400 miles and a bomb capacity of 2,000 pounds if the plane was modified to rid itself of excess weight.

The planes were quickly transformed and the officers and crew, all volunteers, were picked for an "extremely hazardous duty against an unspecified target." On March 1, 1942, the crews began intensive training at Elgin Air Force Field in Florida. Three weeks were spent learning how to take off from a carrier and how to fly at low level and at night. On March 14, 1942, the planes flew to Alameda to join the *Hornet.* On April 1, 1942, April Fools Day, 16 planes were tied to the carrier's deck.

"Sir, the naval aide said, "another message from the *Hornet.*"

"Read it, please."

"Sighted by Japanese picket boat, 650 miles from Japan. Assumed attack warning was signaled before we sank the picket ship. Launched all planes."

"Thank you. Please go."

The President was quiet as he considered the latest information. Turning to Stimson, he said, "They're on their way. God help them."

A few days later, the world learned about the "Doolittle Raid" on Japan and what Americans would call "thirty seconds over Tokyo." The attack caused negligible material damage to Japan, but it did succeed in boosting morale at home, while causing the Japanese to rethink their vulnerability to American attacks. The Home Islands were no longer immune. War had come home to Tokyo.

The humiliated Japanese High Command vowed never to let this happen again. It also sought revenge for the national embarrassment. With emotions running high, the decision was made to confront the Americans in a do-or-die fleet encounter. In time, history would record this decision as the battle for Midway Island in the Central Pacific, an attack that turned into a decisive rout of the Imperial Japanese Navy.

What could have been said by President Lincoln following General George Meade's victory at Gettysburg, and what was said by Prime Minister Winston Churchill after the battle for air supremacy above England, might have been said by the Japanese High Command following the disaster at Midway: "It is not yet the end of the beginning, but it is the beginning of the end." As with the gray-clad-Confederacy and the gutter thugs running the Nazi regime, Japan's military junta could not forsake eventual victory, regardless of the cost in blood to its people.

And so the war in the Pacific would go on…

Almost unnoticed at the time was the decision by the Imperial Japanese Army to reinstate funds to continue balloon bomb experimentation. The exact reason for this change of heart is not fully known.

B-25 PLANES ON THE USS HORNET'S DECK

THE DOOLITTLE RAID

Chapter 4

THE SCHOOL GIRLS

JANUARY 1944 – S.E. HONSHU

The defenses of the Imperial Empire of Japan were cracking.

The war was going poorly for Japan. Little known island fortresses were crumbling before the might of the United States Navy and the "leathernecks," who were assaulting one landing beach after another.

Defeats were everywhere. The "banzai cry" was collapsing before the guns of the West.

The agony began with Guadalcanal and continued into the Solomon Islands and New Guinea. Australia was no longer threatened and Rabaul, Japan's mightiest fortress in the Pacific had fallen. As if climbing a ladder, the American Navy was leap frogging across the largest ocean in the world. The Marshall Islands were gone. The Caroline Islands were gone. The Marianas were threatened, especially the islands of Guam, Saipan, and Tinian. If lost, these three pieces of Pacific real estate would become air bases from which Japan proper would be the target of a bomber onslaught, and from which the country's last island possessions would be truly threatened, the Philippines, Iwo Jima, and Okinawa.

Tokyo's dreams of conquest were crumbling.

Lost in the carnage was a determined undertaking north of Tokyo, where the Imperial Japanese Army was conducting the final experimentation with a balloon bomb. The project's commander, Major General Sueyoski Kusaba had been given the go-ahead by a no longer deaf High Command to commence work with all possible speed. In turn, Major Teiti Takada had forged ahead to resolve all still difficult challenges facing the project. Success had come slowly, but it had come.

The renewed trial release of 200 balloons was scheduled within a month. Radio transmitters in the trial balloons would determine if the balloons, weighted down with equipment and bombs, could use the jet stream to attack the United States.

In his office, though exhausted, the Major General was rereading for the tenth time Teiji's latest report on abortive assaults on the United States.

PART A – PREVIOUS EFFORTS TO ATTACK AMERICA

THE ELLWOOD INCIDENT – On February 23, 1942, the I-17 submarine fired on the Ellwood oil field just west of Goleta, California, a few miles north of the city of Santa Barbara. Beyond hitting the pump house, little damage was done. The I-17's captain, Nisaino Kozo, however, over stated the situation by informing Tokyo that Santa Barbara was in flames. At the most, the attack only caused a short-term invasion scare along the West Coast.

THE ESTEVAN POINT INCIDENT – On June 20, 1942, the I-26 under the command of Yokota Minoru, fired 25 to 30 5-inch shells at the Estevan Point Lighthouse on Vancouver Island in British Columbia. No targets were hit. This was the first and last attack on Canadian soil since the War of 1812.

THE PORT STEVENS INCIDENT –On June 21 and 22, 1942, the I-25, commanded by Tagami Meiji, fired on Fort Stevens at the mouth of the Columbia River. Little damage was done beyond destroying the backstop on the baseball diamond and a few phone lines. This proved to be the only attack on a military base on the US mainland to date.

LOOKOUT AIR RAID INCIDENT – On September 9, 1942, the I-25 launched a E14Y floatplane.. The plane's pilot was Nobuo Fujita. He dropped two 180-pound incendiary bombs over Mt. Emily, near Brookings, Oregon just north of the California border. Unfortunately, no forest fires were started by this effort. To date, this was the only aerial bombing attack on the US mainland.

Kusaba put down the report.. He thought to himself, futile attempts, tiny pin pricks against a giant. What was done at Pearl Harbor could not be done again. There would be only one "December 7th." Something new was needed to terrify the American people into suing for peace, thus permitting Japan to survive the war. Something new was needed to push the Americans away from their position of "unconditional surrender." He turned again to the report.

PART B – OBSTACLES OVERCOME

Building the first air bags for the balloon bombs had proven difficult. Eventually, the bags were made out of paper derived from the "kozo bush." The material was known as "washi paper." Small squares about the size of a road map were pasted together with glue called "konnyaku-non." It is made from a Japanese potato commonly known as the "Devil's Tongue." The washi paper has proved to be very strong, almost impermeable. It was the perfect material for a bag, which would be 33 feet in diameter. Construction of the bags was done so far in large rooms such as concert halls and wrestling venues. Much of the work had been done by high school girls.. Due to the delicacy of the work, long fingernails were not permitted, nor were sharp hairpins. The girls had been told they were working on a secret project to help the country. Their parents had been kept in the dark. The girls were doing a fine job, though they were sometimes scolded for eating the paste, since they were so hungry.

Hungry teenagers thought the base commander. This is what our glorious military has come to, children eating paste to stay alive. He recalled an interview he had done with one of the students two days earlier. Her name was Tanaka Tetsuko. She had felt overwhelmed talking with the gruff and formal military base commander. He had picked her name at random to see how the bag construction was coming.

"What school do you attend?"
"The Yamaguchi Girl's High School, Sir."
"How old are you?"
"Fifteen."
"You are working on the balloon bags?"
"Yes."
"Where?
"In our school gymnasium."
"What have you been told about this project?"
"We are part of a special Student Attack Force."
"And?"
"Working on the bags will help our nation."
"Do you know how?"
"Not exactly."
"What do you think?"
"I … the girls think the bags are for air balloons."
"For what purpose?"
"Balloons to carry bombs, we think, to attack our enemies."
"You figured this out on your own?"
"Yes. What other purpose can the bags have?
"Have you told your parents what you're doing?"
"No. We have been told to keep the work a secret."
"What do your parents think?"
"They think I work with a lot of glue, since it gets on my clothes."

Poor child, he thought, reduced to eating glue to survive.

Stabilizing the air bags was the next biggest challenge. Since the bag was filled with hydrogen, it would be affected by pressure changes caused by changes in temperature due to daytime heating and nighttime cooling. The air bag could not ascend higher than 38,000 feet or fall lower than 30,000 feet. Those were the optimum elevations for it over 60 plus hour trip from Japan to the West Coast.

To prevent the air bag from flying too high, a valve was attached to the bag, which would vent or bleed off hydrogen gas to maintain the proper altitude. If the bag cooled too much, two sandbags would be automatically dropped to achieve the same purpose. Thirty-two sandbags were attached to each air bag.

The balloon's elevation was controlled. This was done by the use an altimeter. Due to the pressure changes, the air bag would go up and down as the altimeter automatically kept the bag on a generally steady course, eastward toward the enemy. The altimeter controlled ballast on the balloon. If the balloon descended below 30,000 feet, a charge was electrically fired to jettison sandbags. With less ballast, the balloon rose. When the balloon rose above 38,000 feet, the altimeter activated a valve to vent hydrogen. This had the effect of lowering the balloon.

THE SANDBAG MECHANISM

The basket would carry 1,000 pounds of gear and contain 19,000 cubic feet of hydrogen (See Diagram, Page 29). The gear included a large, nasty bomb and two or more incendiary charges. More dangerous than this relatively small arsenal, was the possible use of the balloons for biological weapons. The Imperial Army's Noborito Institute cultivated anthrax and cowpox viruses to infect the American population. Military planners were prepared to use biological weapons in early 1944. Emperor Hirohito restrained the Imperial Army and forbade the deployment of such weapons. This was the same decision made by Nazi Germany and the Allies during the war.

After three days of travel, the sand bags would be exhausted and the air bag would drop below 27,500 feet at which time, the loaded bomb and incendiaries would be automatically dropped. Gunpowder flashes would see to this. A second gunpowder flash would occur when the bag was on the ground in order to destroy it. There would be no evidence for the Americans to look at if all worked as planned.

The Major General put down the report. Teiti and his group had done an outstanding job given their limited resources and the time constraints placed on them. He was sincerely proud of the engineers working on the base. The Navy provided a "Type B Balloon." It was 30 feet in diameter and made from rubberized silk. This balloon was used mainly for meteorological purposes. They were also used to determine the possibility of the bomb balloons reaching the American coastline. The bomb balloons evolved from the Navy's prototype. The release of 200 balloons to check the effectiveness of balloon bombs would take place soon. Of that, he was most certain. Tokyo was demanding the test. If successful, the High Command wanted 100,000 balloon bombs constructed.

What concerned Kusaba was not how to build so many balloons, but when the first air attacks on America would begin. Tokyo had not provided a date. He knew in his heart that another "event" was necessary to push the military strategists. He knew with absolute certainty that moment awaited the next American attack, which this time, he concluded, would be heavy and continuous aerial bombings of Japan. The "Doolittle Raid" was only a slight harbinger of what was about to befall the country. The existence of the new American B-29 had changed everything. He took no joy in his conclusion.

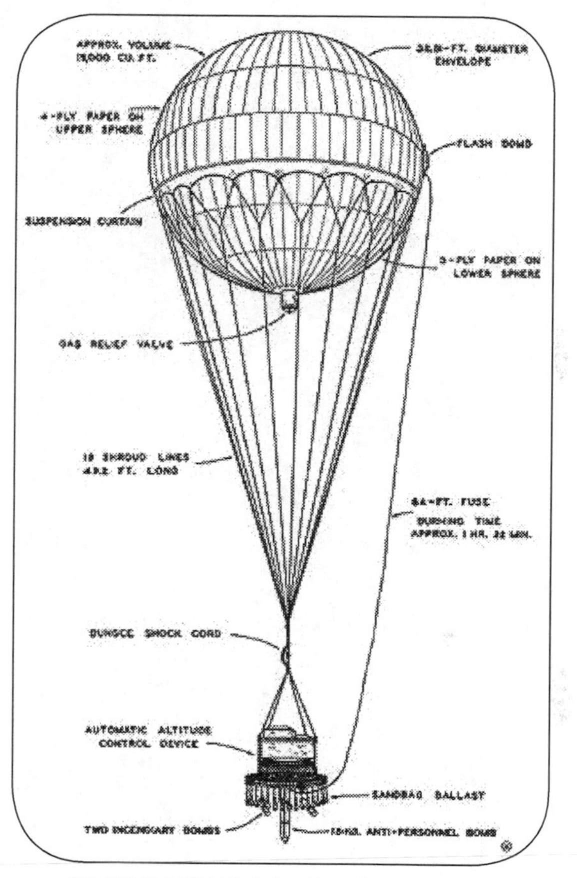

SKETCH OF THE BALLOON BOMB

Chapter 5

THE INFERNO

MARCH 1945 – THE PACIFIC THEATER

The plane's engines roared to life in the middle of the night, sputtering at first, than purring with a consistent drone seeking to break the last restraints which still fastened it to the airfield. The noise was overwhelming, four great engines turning over a 2,200 horsepower each. The smell of exhaust fumes permeated the night air and added to the tenseness of the crews and officers already aboard, who would fly and fight in the great plane on its mission to end the war. It was not alone in this endeavor. Over 300 planes were preparing to take-off under a quiet full moon and the glow of distant stars. With eleven men to each plane, over 3,500 young men would take to the skies in their giant B-29's.

It was their time to change history.

It would take a few hours for the vast air armada to take off, and then more than six long hours to reach their target at dawn on March 9, 1945. The planes, of course, were unaware of the mission's purpose or their own rationale for existence. They simply responded to their masters and poured down the many runways on Tinian Island and lifted into the night skies.

In time, the planes gathered themselves at 30,000 feet and began the long run to Japan. No one had ever seen anything like this before in history. The Super-fortresses were 90 feet long, nose to tail. The tail itself was 27 feet high or about the height of a three-story building. Wingtip to wingtip, the span was 171 feet. The plane had two bomb bays and could carry a payload exceeding 20,000 pounds. The four great engines drove the planes in excess of 350 m.p.h.

The bomb load was impressive, frighteningly so. For this mission, the armada carried over 700,000 incendiary bombs, which were called M-69's. Each M-69 weighed exactly six pounds and was dropped in clusters of 38 within an individual container. Each B-29 carried 37 containers. Each plane, therefore, held over 1,400 incendiaries. Once dropped, the cluster container automatically opened at 5,000 feet to release the payload. The incendiaries would explode on contact with the ground and spread a jelly-petrol compound, which was highly flammable. Whatever it touched would burn.

The first planes to reach Japan were the "pathfinders," the B-29's that would drop napalm bombs every 100 feet across the city to mark the targets. And then the bombers would come in staggered formations and various elevations between 8,000 and 10,000 feet. The powerful warring planes would take three hours to fly over the city which they had come to destroy by "carpet bombing" it. This was not strategic bombing, where specific buildings, war plants, and military installations were targeted in order to reduce civilian casualties. The sole purpose of this mission was to create a "fire storm," to devour the city in flames and break the will of its people to continue the war.

There was precedent for this mission. The "blitz" of London by the Nazi two-engine Junkers had tried to bomb a city into submission and great fires had been started, but not a hellish firestorm. That was something entirely new. It came with the attack on Hamburg in August 1943 when the British Royal Air Force gained payback. Great waves of British bombers ignited numerous fires in the city, which eventually combined into one uncontrollable mass of flame. The fire was so hot it generated its own self-sustaining winds of gale-force intensity. The oxygen was sucked out of the air, causing people to suffocate. The heat was so great that river and canal water boiled, and people literally exploded from the terrible temperatures.

The British raid on Hamburg had unintentionally caused a firestorm. The American raid on Japan was seeking to intentionally cause such an inferno. It was a time of retribution for the Pearl Harbor attack.

The American High Command anticipated and projected that 15 to 16 miles of the Tokyo would be leveled, destroyed beyond immediate repair. Over 16 major industrial areas and factories would be eliminated. Some 250,000 or more buildings would be burned to the ground. At least 100,000 people would be killed and another 100,000 injured. At least 300000 people would be homeless. As in Hamburg, the fire would consume the oxygen and people would suffocate. There would be no safety in the boiling rivers. The fire would consume all in its path. The projections made were conservative.

In preparation for the attack, an entire Japanese town had been built in Utah. It was called the "Dugway Project." An architect, Antonio Raymond, who had studied in Japan for eighteen years, was given the assignment of replicating a typical Japanese locale: streets, buildings, and the actual construction materials. Used in Japan. The town was built to precise specifications in order to determine the effectiveness of bombs and incendiary devices; that is, to determine what was needed to create a firestorm.

The morality of the raid was, of course debated in the White House and the Pentagon by war planners. The ultimate argument came down to this. Many, both Japanese and Americans, would be killed now to avoid killing even more later. Many would be sacrificed today to save others tomorrow. The deaths of so many would shorten the war.

If this came to pass, the Tokyo fire raid would accomplish a justifiable goal. If the war continued, more B-29 raids would rain destruction on a nation almost defenseless against the B-29's.

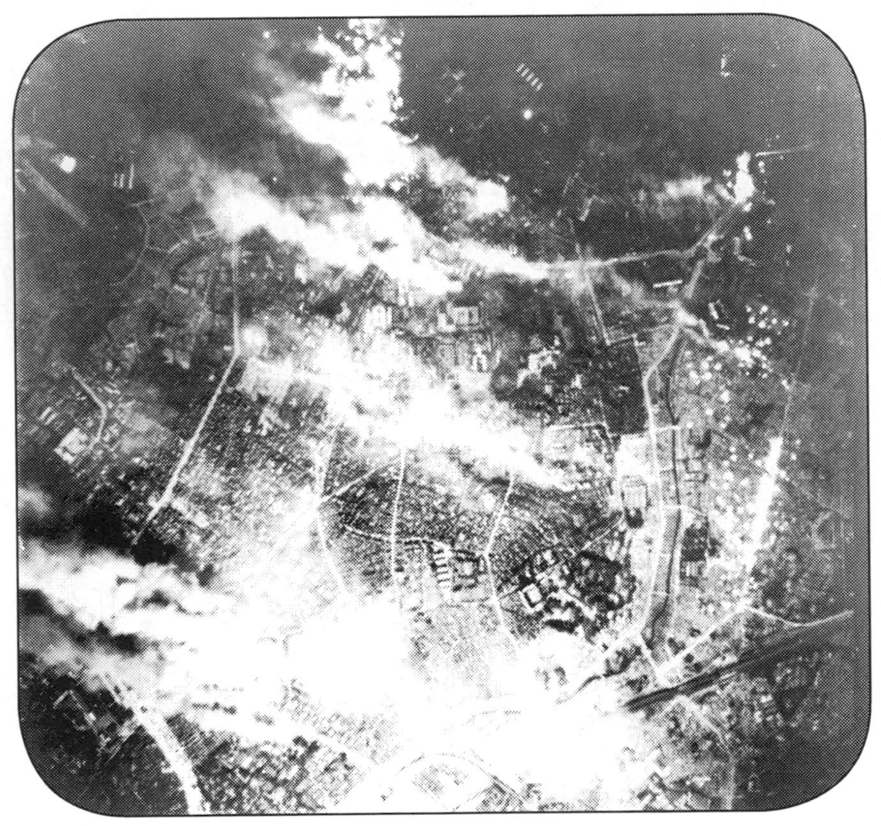

THE TOKYO FIRESTORM

Chapter 6

STRANGE OCCURRENCES

<u>1945 – In the Air</u>

"Look at that, off to the port side," the navigator said with a surprised tone to his voice."

"What the hell are those?" the radio officer asked, equally curious about what was passing a mere 1,000 feet below the B-29.

"They look like giant mushrooms floating in the air," the gun controller said, perhaps a bit too loudly.

The B-29, one of 300, was at 32,000 feet on its westerly flight to Japan from the island of Tinian. Below were balloons, so many of them, leisurely floating eastward in the jet stream. The two armadas passed each other, almost close enough to touch, at least metaphorically. This was the Pacific air war in the waning months of 1945.

"I wonder where they're headed?" the pilot wondered aloud.

"And where did they come from?" the co-pilot responded.

1945 – At Sea

The lookouts aboard the destroyer, approximately fifty miles west of Hawaii were the first to see the object.

"About two-hundred yards ahead. Looks like a giant sheet, a huge piece of white cloth dragging something. It doesn't look like a mine."

The destroyer slowed as it approached the mysterious item bobbing in the swells. All hands were alert.

"Looks like a balloon, a damn big one, " the Captain said. "That basket those lines are attached to… No telling what's that all about. Let's bypass it, whatever it is."

"Why would that thing be out here?" a Chief remarked to no one in particular. Maybe it's a weather balloon."

APRIL – 1945 – THE WEST COAST

A family enjoying a Sunday picnic in Los Angeles' Griffith Park discovered bits of washi paper in a meadow. The paper seemed to have some sort of glue on it. Eventually, the military authorities were told about the discovery. Strangely, they didn't seem all that surprised.

Earlier in the year, a number of people returning from a party in the wee hours of the morning claimed to have seen a giant balloon floating high above Santa Monica. Though they had enjoyed a few drinks, they insisted their powers of observation remained untouched. A strikingly full moon had cast light on the balloon for a minute or so before drifting clouds obscured their view. Again, the authorities learned about this experience. And again, they seemed unsurprised by the report.

Near Medford, Oregon in the southern part of the state, an explosion took place in a forested area. Police investigators could find no cause for the blast. They did, however, come across shreds of paper in the immediate area of the explosion and the small fire that it started. As might be expected, the local police contacted the FBI, which in turn spoke to the West Coast Military Command. Once more, the investigators seemed to take the incident in stride.

Two men were perched on a old rusty pickup truck, which was parked near the rugged north coastline of Japan. They were drinking hot tea from metal cups to ward off the early morning chill. Their muscles were stiff was the long hours they had spent watching balloons released.

"That's the last of them," the Major said, "almost 9,000 balloons are now on their journey to our enemy."

"Teiji, you have done your job well," the Major General said with obvious pride in his voice. "You made the impossible possible."

"We should be sending 100,000 balloons to our American friends, Sir."

"What we would like to do and what we can do," the older man said with resignation in his voice, "are two different things."

"If the B-29's hadn't destroyed our hydrogen manufacturing plants..."

"But they did, and most of Tokyo and too many other cities."

"How can they rain death on our people, innocent civilians? They must be monsters."

General Kusaba's answer shook his young understudy. "They can do it because they want to, Teiji, just as we do with our balloons."

On November 5, 1944, a Coast Guard Reserve patrol boat discovered an unusual object off the California coast --- a gummed paper bag attached to what looked like a large bicycle wheel with Japanese markings on it. A hurried call to the military authorities eventually brought the find to the Pentagon's attention. This time everyone was surprised.

On January 10, 1945, near the small rural community of Alturas in northeast California not far from the Oregon border, two forest rangers spotted a balloon drifting high over the nearby forests. They reported the sighting to the military and shortly thereafter an Army P-38 fighter plane was dispatched to shoot the balloon down. This it did. The wounded balloon descended slowly over Tule Lake in plain sight of, ironically enough, the Japanese Relocation Camp in the area. The balloon finally came to rest in trees on a mountain slope 30 miles from Alturas.

Investigators found the paper balloon in remarkable good condition. It was still intact. Slung to a wheel were four incendiary bombs and one high explosive bomb. Everything was sent to Moffett Field in Sunnyvale, where a complete examination was done, including reflating the balloon and test flying it.

Eventually, the balloon would be given to the Smithsonian National Air Museum after the war.

"We must fight on," Teiji said with the stubbornness of youth. "We cannot surrender to the Americans."

"Oh, we will fight," the Major General said. "It is in our blood, our history. But in the end, we will surrender."

"Sir!"

"We cannot win. The Americans are too strong."

"Look what we did to them on Iwo Jima. We bled them."

"Yes, our troops fought well and the Marines paid dearly. But, Teiji, what flag now flies about the island?"

"We will fight them on Okinawa."

"We will, but in the end it will be the same. This war is lost."

The small town of Hayfork is located in northern California about 40 miles west of Redding. A Japanese balloon was observed on February 1, 1945. It was slowly drifting over the Trinity National Forest and the balloon was descending.

No one knew what it was. An alert forest ranger called the military at the Presidio in San Francisco and reported the sighting. In the meantime, the balloon came to rest atop a 60-foot dead fir tree in the forest near a local road used by lumberjacks. Word spread and soon many people gathered in the area to gaze up at the strange object. They continued staring, if not gawking, into the early evening, when, shortly after the sun went down, there was a tremendous blast.

The balloon's control box had worked perfectly. The big gasbag disappeared in a fireball and the wheel undercarriage came crashing down to the ground. Though it was difficult to believe, no one was hurt. Forest rangers quickly sealed off the immediate area to keep the curious well back from the fallen debris until Army personnel arrived. After examination, it was determined that the balloon destruction mechanism had worked as programmed, thereby causing the hydrogen to explode. Fortunately, however, the attached bomb and incendiaries had not ignited.

The local people were told what the balloon was and were asked to keep the secret they had seen.

On March 10, 1945, the government received a real scare. A balloon descended in Washington State in the vicinity of Hanford, where the Manhattan Project was located. The balloon landed on a power line that fed electricity to the reactor building producing plutonium for the Nagasaki bomb. The reactor was shut down until the power line was repaired.

The irony of the moment was all too evident.

"Sir, our 'kamikaze planes' will destroy their fleet."

"Some ships, yes, Teiji, but not their fleet."

"Our young men fly with the Emperor's spirit."

"The Americans," the Major General said, "bring with them a spirit too, which we ignited at Pearl Harbor."

"Are you a defeatist, Sir."
"I'm a realist."
"Our balloons..."
"Will change nothing."
"Had we placed biological germs in them..."
"Not even our German allies crossed that line."
"You are saying there are rules in war?"
"There are none in war. There are only temptations."
"I don't understand."
"You are young. In time you will."
"If we survive."
"We will, Teiji. Now tell me again the beautiful words you said when the balloons were released. They were so poetic."

The balloons were visible for several minutes after release, then they faded away as a spot in the blue sky like a daytime star.

"You have the heart of a poet. Survive this tragedy and share your heart with our people. They will need beautiful words."

May 5, 1945 came to America in the midst of the Okinawa campaign, a bloody island campaign only 600-miles from the home islands of Japan. The bitterness of war was brought home by the absolute refusal of the defenders to surrender to the Marines. A slaughter was taking place on both sides.

In the back of everyone's mind was a painful question, the answer to which was all too easily seen. What would happen when the United States invaded Japan in 1946? How great would the carnage be?

On this day, though, on a sweet Sunday, the Rev. Archie Mitchell, who was the minister of the Christian Alliance Church in Bly, Oregon, took his pregnant wife and five church children on a picnic. They drove for a time before finding a beautiful shady spot about 16 miles into the mountains. The kids, mainly teens, scampered out of the car and, along with Mrs. Mitchell, looked for the ideal place to picnic. As they did, Rev. Mitchell parked his car in a nearby shady spot close to the exit road. As he left his car to bring the lunches to the kids and his wife, he heard someone yell, "I've found a balloon." The minister had heard about the Japanese bomb balloons and yelled to the kids to leave it alone, not to touch it. He was too late.

One of the curious children touched or tugged on the balloon. That was all it took to detonate one of the bombs the balloon carried. The resulting blast killed Mrs. Mitchell and all the children. The explosion was so great it plowed up the ground and virtually destroyed the balloon.

Two nearby forest service employees heard the bomb going off and immediately joined the dazed and shocked minister. They covered the bodies and took Rev. Mitchell to Bly, the nearest town.

The dead would later be removed from their isolated, yet lovely picnic area. Though Mr. Mitchell could not know it at the time, years later a monument would be placed where the balloon bomb exploded to remember the only Americans killed during the balloon campaign. The names of the children were listed.

Elsie Mitchell, 26
Sherman Shoemaker, 12
Jay Gifford, 12
Eddie Engen, 13
Joan Patzke 11
Dick Patzke 13

The Mitchell tragedy was reported in a most succinct manner lacking in any human emotion. An unidentified object had exploded, killing six people. A week earlier, it was later revealed the Japanese were releasing balloons into the wind currents, which were carrying them across the Pacific. The public was strongly warned to avoid touching them. Rev. Mitchell had understood the warning. One of the children had not. Years later a monument was erected in memory of the tragedy.

THE MITCHELL MONUMENT

The Undersecretary of War, William Peterson later made the following statement concerning the Bly case.

This was the only known casualty or damage from the paper balloons and added that any further damage must be kept under strict censorship to prevent the Japanese from learning how effective the balloons had become.

Balloons have been found over most of the western mainland. They are gray, white, or greenish-blue paper, about 33 feet in diameter, and carry a few ball bombs suspended beneath the balloon. It was one of these bombs which had failed to explode when the balloon landed about 30 miles north of the California-Oregon border, and more than 200 miles from the ocean in the Fremont National Forest.

The bomb had lain undiscovered for some time in the woods and warned that there would be others found as snow melts and vacationers go into the mountains and the back country.

Censorship is always a key part of any war effort. The questions is always what to censor? In the case of the balloons, the Office of Censorship tried to keep the lid on the threat caused by the balloon bombs. The government feared a panic on the West Coast if people connected the balloons to possible biological warfare. This was especially difficult when *Newsweek Magazine* ran an article entitled, "Balloon Mystery" (January 1,1945). Newspapers and radio stations were immediately asked to avoid mentioning the story. The tragedy of Oregon, however, resulted in a temporary stay in order to warn the public without causing widespread panic. This was particularly true in the case of biological warfare.

Within the government there was a hot debate as to the release point for the balloons. No one thought they came from Japan. Some believed the balloons were released from Japanese submarines lurking off the West Coast. Others, given to crazy rumors, maintained the balloons were released from Japanese Relocation Camps in the United States, or, even more outlandishly, from POW camps housing captured German soldiers in southern states. In time reason prevailed. Samples of the sand from the balloon's sandbags were analyzed. The military geological unit of the US Geological Service did the analysis. After a considerable chemical examination of the sand, the geologists determined the precise Japanese beach used for their balloon campaign.

There is a last irony concerning the Mitchell tragedy. A few weeks later, on the Wilson Ranch near Yerington, Nevada, a group of cowboys discovered a balloon, which they called the "Emperor's puffballs." They tied it to the rear bumper of their car and dragged it to a garage on the ranch. Attempts to reach the authorities led to nothing. They were stuck with the balloon and its weapons. With uncommon courage or a complete disregard for life and limb, they deflated the balloon and used it to cover a haystack. The two bombs never went off.

Had the children from Bly found this balloon, how things might have been different.

"Sir, what will you do after the war?"
"Teiji, perhaps I will write a book about our project. And you?"
"Maybe I'll return to civil engineering, my first love."

"There should be lots of work. The entire country will have to be rebuilt."

"The Americans will do this?"

"We will be their new ally."

"What?"

"The Nazi government is defeated leaving Russia a powerful victor in Europe and Asia. In time there will be a confrontation between two superpowers, the American eagle and the Russian bear."

"And?"

"We will join hands with our former enemy."

"I can't believe that."

"Believe it. It is the way of the world."

The two men were silent now as they looked out at an empty sky and the vast, turbulent waters of the Pacific. Out there, on beaches and at sea, the future of their country was being played out. The clash of arms would determine everything. Already, they perceived the outcome of that battle and what the days ahead would bring. Teiji broke their silence.

"Sir, I wonder how many balloons actually got to America?"

Military historians believed that over 9,000 balloons were released. Of that number, 30 were shot down either by fighter planes or anti-aircraft guns. About 100 balloons were found during the war after they landed. Slightly more than 150 balloons were discovered after the war along the West Coast, and as far east as Michigan, as far south as Mexico, and as far north as the Yukon Territory. The best estimates suggest that 1,000 balloons crossed the Pacific successfully and that 700 or more have never been found.

Out there somewhere in the forests and mountains of the west were many undiscovered and unexploded balloons waiting to be found. This would be especially true along the California-Oregon border.

BALLOON BOMB ON THE GROUND

Chapter 7

MEMORIES

Perspectives

Robert Guillain was a French reporter assigned to Japan in 1938. He stayed on in Japan after war broke out in Europe and was trapped in Japan after the attack on Pearl Harbor. Fortunately, he survived the war and returned to France once hostilities ceased.

He was in Tokyo on the night of March 9, 1945 when the B-29's made their low level attack on the city. In 1981, he wrote a book entitled, *I Saw Tokyo Burning.* The quotes that follow came from his book.

The incendiaries scattered a kind of flaming dew that skittered along the roofs, setting fire to everything they splashed and spreading a wash of dancing flames everywhere.

Roofs collapsed under the bombs' impact and within minutes the frail houses of wood and paper were aflame, lighted from the inside like paper lanterns. The hurricane-force wind puffed up great clots of flame and sent burning planks flying through the air to fell people and set fire to what they touched. Flames from a distant cluster of houses would suddenly spring up close at hand, traveling at the speed of a forest fire. Then screaming families abandoned their homes; sometimes the women had already left, carrying their babies and dragging crates or mattresses. Too late: the circle of fire had closed off their street. Sooner or later, everyone was surrounded by fire.

Wherever there was a canal, people hurled themselves into the water; in shallow places, people waited, half sunk in noxious muck, mouths just above the surface of the water. Hundreds of them were later found dead; not drowned, but asphyxiated by the burning air and smoke. In other places, the water got so hot that the luckless bathers were simply boiled alive.

As panic brought ever-fresh waves of people pressing into the narrow strips of land, those in front were pushed irresistibly toward the river; whole walls of screaming humanity toppled over and disappeared in the deep water. Thousands of drowned bodies were later recovered from the Sumida estuary.

In 1944 Tanaka Tetsuko was fifteen years old. She was attending a local high school when a Japanese officer spoke to her class.

He told us we would be making a "secret weapon." The weapon would have a great impact on the war. He didn't say then that we would be making balloon bombs, only that somehow what we made would fly to America.

A factory started at our school in August 1944. Stands were placed all over the schoolyard and drying boards were erected on them. We covered the board with a thin layer of paste … and then laid down two sheets of Japanese paper and brushed out any bubbles. When dry, a thicker layer of paste, with a slightly bluish hue, a little like the color of the sky, was evenly applied to it. The process was repeated five times.

We really believed we were doing secret work, so I didn't talk about this even at home, but my clothes were covered with paste, so my family must have been able to figure out something.

Tanaka Tetsuko survived the war. She later learned what the secret project was that she had worked on as a student.

We only learned some forty years later that the balloon bombs were made had actually reached America. They started a few forest fires and inflicted some casualties, among the children. Five children and a woman on a picnic in Oregon in May 1945 were killed when a bomb dropped earlier exploded. When I heard that, I was stunned. I made those weapons… Some of us got together and felt we would like to organize an effort to apologize.

I started with my classmates but encountered strong resistance.

In the last analysis, what can be said? The war in the Pacific was a fire that consumed all.

JAPANESE SCHOOLGIRLS CONSTRUCTING A BALLOON

Part II

THE CCC

THE FIRST NEW DEAL C.C.C. CAMP

Chapter 8

GRANDPA

MARCH 1966 – SAN FRANCISCO

Matt Samuels was in a hurry. He gripped the wheel of his red-maroon Ford pickup and tapped the gas pedal ever so lightly to push his speed up just a bit more than the posted m.p.h. He wanted to get to the V.A. Hospital fast, but not at the expense of a speeding ticket. To a degree, he was a master at this, as were most of his high school buddies. Speed, but don't make it obvious was their mantra. It gave them a thrill without breaking a leg."

The V.A. Hospital was located in the Richmond District of San Francisco, clearly a long way from where Matt lived in the Diamond Heights area of the city. Still, he made good time and parked a few minutes before the morning visiting hours began. As he walked toward the hospital, he churned over in his head what had led him to this visit.

It all began in February when the spring semester --- and his last high school semester --- began. He was urged by his counselor to take a college class at City College of San Francisco (CCSF) while completing his high school graduation requirements. Mrs. Collins had called it a concurrent program, where he would attend two different schools, and get both high school credits and college units. It seemed like a smart things to do.

He enrolled in U.S. History 170, a survey course of contemporary American History from 1900 to the present. Matt was not inclined to study the Puritans, colonial America, or the Revolution. While he liked traveling in the West, he wasn't into America's frontier history. In short, he needed to be current, up-to-date. This class met his needs.

But what he didn't count on was a research paper, a requirement that constituted a major portion of his final grade. That led him to a talk with his father.

"Dad, I signed up. U.S. History."

"Nice. You should learn something about our country," his dad said with a chuckle.

"We have to write a research paper."

"You make it sound like a death sentence, Matt."

"I was hoping to ease through my last semester."

"But you do get college credit. Mrs. Collins pointed that out."

"Yeah."

"But?"

"I need a topic. You're a reporter. Give me some ideas."

"Ideas?"

Robert Samuels checked out his son. Tall and good looking, very athletic and smart, Matt was a cool kid. He just hated to write, though, of course, he could and did so well when he put his mind to it. The trick now was to encourage him without appearing to assist too much.

"Well, you could write about the *Aaron Ward*, Matt."

"Nay, dad, you took care of that with your book, *Miracle at RPS 10."*

"What about the Korean War?"

"You covered it with another book, *Miracle at Pusan*."

"I did, didn't I? Okay, what about the Four Chaplains? And before you say anything, remember you did some research about their heroism."

"You covered the subject with *The Miracle of the Fifth Chaplain*."

"It would seem, son, that we need another miracle."

"A topic, Pop."

Samuels loved it when Matt called him "Pop." It always sounded amusing and friendly, certainly very informal with more than a little smattering of affection adorning the word. Now he needed to come through for the kid.

"I've got it."

"What?"

"Before you say no, hear me out."

"No promises."

"None required."

"Go for it."

"Why not research and write about the CCC, the Civilian Conservation Corps, which your grandfather was in for two years during the Great Depression."

"The 1930's?"

"Yes."

"I don't know."

"Think about it, Matt. You could do your library research, and then, and this is the neat part, you might interview your grandfather. That's called living history."

"But he's in the hospital."

"No way around it, Matt. His heart is giving out, but he's still kicking and I know he would love to talk about his experiences at Arroyo Grande."

"Where's that?"

"It's a small town down the coast, a few miles from Morro Rock?"

"Where's that?"

"I'll get you a map. Now, what do you think?

"A tentative yes. I want to check out the topic before I make a commitment."

"Good lad. Caution is a healthy virtue."

Matt checked out the topic. He did considerable research in the local libraries at San Francisco State and City College. And that's how he came to the VA Hospital one early morning in March. He was here for an interview.

He found his grandfather in Ward 7. It was the ward for old guys with heart problems for the most part. Most of them were vets of World War II or Korea, and now a new group of young-old men from Vietnam. As Matt would soon see, every bed had a patient.

Instead of finding his grandfather in bed, Matt found him sitting at a small table in the attached recreation room. On the table there were a number of scrapbooks. His grandfather had changed out of his hospital togs and was wearing a dark blue short-sleeved shirt and light blue pants. True to his habits, he wore an old pair of black, heavily shined loafers. As always, he wasn't wearing socks. He looked rather snappy. Matt thought his complexion seemed healthier than the last time they had met, when he first entered the hospital, a few weeks earlier. In fact, he looked downright good for a guy who had recently been playing tag with a coronary. Seeing him, his grandfather gave his usual greeting to his grandson, "How yah doing, kid?" Matt returned the greeting with a big smile and a hearty, "Great, Grandpa."

"Good to see you, Kid." He always used that term, "kid," but not as a put down. Rather, it was a term of endearment. His grandfather loved the dickens out of him. For his part, Matt always called his grandfather, grandpa. The term invoked the same feelings of affection.

"Have a seat, Kid."
"Right."
"The nurses let me dress up for the occasion. What do you think?"
"Pretty sharp."
"Maybe I can get a date with the cute nurse who comes on later."
"Grandpa."
"Don't grandpa me. I'm not that old and the old ticker is still ticking away like a Timex at the bottom of the ocean."
"Well, give her a kiss for me."
"The hell, I will. Get your own date. By the way, how's that little cheerleader you've been dating?"
She's cool."
"I'll take that as terrific, which is what I think she is, Kid."

Matt shifted the topic. "Grandpa, you know why I'm here."

"Because you love me?"

"That, too.

"I know, kid, and I'm ready for the inquisition."

"Interview."

"Whatever. You've done some research, I hear, and I've got my scrapbooks. Let's get at it. There's a lot to talk about."

"Where should we start, Grandpa?"

"How about March 21, 1933.

On that day I was broke. I was flat on my back. Three years of the Great Depression had wiped me out, and then some. Try this on for size. In 1929, I had $600 in the bank. Then came the stock market crash, and the banks were right behind. There was a "run" on First National. I got ten cents on the dollar --- $60 lousy bucks. We didn't have FDIC in those days. We just had people going crazy trying to get their money out of the bank. Believe me, it was a mob scene. People were pushing and shoving in line. The cops at the bank's doors had their hands full. Inside the bank, it was chaotic. People were screaming and cursing the tellers, and yelling threats into the high heavens. One guy was dragged away for pulling a ten-inch knife out in order to make his withdrawal.

I was out of work. There was no work on the wharf, where I had worked as a longshoreman. My old part time job with the Post Office was gone. Washing dishes in a downtown hotel wasn't a very lucrative job, but it was better than working in the beer plant scrubbing out the brewing tanks. I didn't have a nickel to my name. I couldn't, as they say, "beg, borrow, or steal" a job. I couldn't take care of your grandmother and your father. It was the pits.

I had voted for Herbert Hoover in '28. I didn't hold him personally responsible for the terrible depression. But I did hold him to the fire for not helping those out of work --- the 15-millon of us who were unemployed. We needed jobs. In 1932 I cast my lot with Roosevelt. He won and I hoped for the best. I knew little about him. He had been Governor of New York and was from upstate, some place called Hyde Park. I liked the music the Democrats were singing. *"Happy days are here again..."*

Turns out, it was a good vote. Roosevelt won by a landslide. On March 21, 1933, Roosevelt went before the Congress, and I quote from my scrapbook:

"I propose to create a civilian conservation corps to be used to in simple work, not interfering with normal employment, and confining itself to forestry, the prevention of soil erosion, flood control, and similar projects. I call your attention to the fact that this type of work is of definite practical value, not only through the prevention of great present financial loss, but also as a means of creating future national wealth."

Interrupting his grandfather, Matt said, "On March 27th, the legislation creating the CCC was passed by the Senate, and three days later by the House of Representatives. The President signed the final bill soon after."

"Very good, Kid. You have done your homework."

"I didn't want to let you down, Grandpa."

"You never have, Kid."

YOUNG MEN AT WORK

I had heard about the program and wanted to sign up. Unfortunately for me, the original CCC was set up for high school and college age boys, 18 – 25. That left me out in the cold. Then I got lucky. On May 11, 1933, after a great deal of robust lobbying by veterans of World War I, things changed. We were permitted to join the CCC under Executive Order 6129. You could be over 25, even married, but you had to be a vet.

Within a few weeks, I was declared eligible by the Veterans Administration and inducted into the CCC. Initially, 28,000 vets signed up. By 1940, over 250,000 vets were in the CCC. That was about 5% of the total number of enrollees.

So I was in… But I had no idea where I would be sent. None at all…

"Sounds like you finally got a break," Matt said.

"At the time, my sentiments, too."

YOUNG CCC RECRUITS

Chapter 9

ARROYO GRANDE

MARCH 1966 – SAN FRANCISCO

"Grandpa, you were sent to Arroyo Grande, right?"

"You got it, kid. By bus from San Francisco with a bunch of other city stiffs like myself, all vets of Mr. Wilson's desire to 'make the world safe for democracy.'"

"Before you ask, Grandpa, I know where it's located. I checked it out on the map."

Grandpa liked his grandson. Good kid, as he was fond of saying. Got lots on the ball. "What else do you know about the town?"

"It's located on the Central Coast in San Luis Obispo county and is part of a five city complex of small towns ---Pismo Beach, Shell Beach, Grover Beach, Oceano, and, of course, Arroyo Grande."

"Pretty good."

"The first European to see the area was Juan Cabrillo, but the first people there were the Chumash Indians. The area has a long Spanish-Mexican heritage. We gained control of it, along with California, during the Bear Flag Rebellion in 1848."

"When I got to Arroyo Grande, it was hardly more than a bus stop. If you blinked, you missed the town. But it would be home for two years."

"Tell me about it, Grandpa."

To begin with, I almost made it to Pine Valley in San Diego County. That's where the first CCC camp was established in California. Along with hundreds of other guys, I was sent to Fort Rosecrans for two weeks of tough conditioning to get myself in shape. That was difficult. City life doesn't really prepare you for hard outdoors work, even if you work the docks slugging it out with heavy crates and bums who wanted your job. Still, I was in better shape than the paper pushers. I was issued a World War I surplus uniform, a shirt, and a pair of boots, plus a mattress filled with straw to be placed in my tent home until barracks could be built. Other structures had to be built, too. We needed a kitchen, mess hall, a recreational hall, office, an infirmary, and a large shed for equipment and general storage. Naturally, we had to build latrines. The camp was under the direction of army officers. Paid civilians supervised the daily work projects.

Robert Fechner headed the national CCC program. He was a former union organizer. President Roosevelt appointed him to establish the rules and regulations for the CCC. This was a smart move by FDR. The White House picked Fechner to avoid union criticism of the program. Many people thought the CCC would take work away from the private sector. Businesses and workers didn't want to compete with the government. Fechner's appointment quieted some of the more vocal criticism.

"I read somewhere, Grandpa, that you were called "bush marines," and "woodpeckers" Any truth to that?"

"To my everlasting dismay, yes."

"Weren't you paid a dollar-a-day?"

"Thirty dollars per month, which was a lot of money in those days. Of course, anyone with a family only kept $5.00. The rest was sent home to keep the wife and kids going. The sawbuck was okay by me."

"Wasn't there controversy about this?"

"The unions wanted a higher wage for CCC workers. They were afraid $1.00 per day might become the prevailing wage for all workers.."

"I can't imagine living on so little."

"Kid, those were different days."

"How many men were in your camp?"

"Forty-eight men and they worked a six day week under the leadership of a LEM."

"A what?"

"A 'local experienced man', who trained us to use tools and heavy equipment, and who supervised our work on projects. A LEM had usually spent a lifetime working in the outdoors. These guys kept us from killing ourselves. Hell, for a while, he was the only one who knew what he was doing."

"Dare I asked, Grandpa, about the food?"

"Dare away. I had three square meals each day. No one went hungry. For breakfast there was lots of oatmeal, bacon and eggs, plus bread and butter, milk, and steaming hot coffee. For lunch frankfurters were king, along with sauerkraut, and boiled potatoes, creamed carrots, and lots of rice pudding. More times than I care to remember, Irish stew, mashed potatoes, and string beans were served at dinner. For dessert, there was always custard pudding. I think we ate better than the regular army. The CCC spent $1.50 per meal. The army spent only forty-five cents. They sure didn't spend much on us when I was on a destroyer. Maybe they thought hungry men would be better fighters."

"All this talk about food is making me hungry, Grandpa."

At that precise moment, two people entered the room. One brought Grandpa's breakfast meal: pancakes, eggs, and sausage for starters, plus juice and coffee. The other person, a very charming nurse, had other things on her mind.

"It's time for the vital signs before you dine."

"Listen young lady, the only vital signs that count are my age, rank, and serial number. In that order, I'm 77, retired, and available tonight to take you to the movies, if your social calendar will permit."

"Nice try, but I'm afraid my husband would object."

"Don't tell him."

"I'll get back to you on that. In the meantime, I need to take your temperature and blood pressure. Any objections?"

"Not for a beautiful gal like you."

"You're such a flirt. All talk, I bet."

"Test me."

Ignoring Grandpa, the nurse took and found his temperature and blood pressure to be OK.

"Who's this?" the young nurse said, pointing to Matt.

"My grandson. You keep your hands off him."

"Your grandpa always this way?" she asked Matt.

"Only when he wants to impress me."

"Don't listen to him beautiful. He's still wet behind the ears."

"But he is cute."

With that the nurse left us.

"She thinks you're cute, Matt."

"Cute! I hate the word."

"Go with the flow."

"Can we get back to the interview?"

"Shoot."

"Grandpa, I read that the CCC had a busy first year. According to the government, 213 miles of firebreaks were put in throughout the country. Over 750 erosion control dams were built. Nearly 600 miles of telephone lines were constructed. At least 850 miles of truck trails were built, and almost the same number of firebreaks were put in to protect the Sierra Nevada Mountains."

"That much? Well, I knew we were working from dawn to dusk. Here's a number for you. The guys in the CCC planted over three billion trees.

That I know. They reforested the darn country, especially the states hit by the "dust bowl. We did other things, too. Over 800 state parks were established. We also worked in all the national parks. Next time you're camping, check for a CCC mark in the area. Check under a park bench. That's a good place to look. I'll bet you tomorrow's pay you'll find triple 'C's.'"

"You guys were all over the place."

"You can say that again, but don't. We stocked rivers and streams with fish. We went after the mosquito and did a lot with flood control and laid miles of drainage pipes. Toward the end of the 1930's, much of the CCC work dealt with improving the infrastructure for military training facilities."

"What about women and minorities? Were they in the CCC, too?"

Matt's grandpa surprised him with his response. "Here, have some of my breakfast. The pancakes looked edible. I'm not sure about the eggs. Sometimes I think there's a cook in this place who wants to kill me before my ticker does. We'll get to your questions on a full stomach. No need to ruin breakfast."

Ruin breakfast! What was grandpa talking about? Matt thought to himself. Why is he avoiding my questions?

At that moment, the charming nurse popped in with another breakfast tray. She quickly deposited it on the bed before winking at Matt. "I found this tray floating around the ward. Matt isn't it? You better eat the evidence before the FBI shows up. There's a major somewhere who's looking for his hot pancakes."

"Will do," Matt yelped out with a big smile. Thanks."

Both men dug into their breakfast with relish. As they did, they turned to small talk, if you want to call it that.

"How's your dad treating you kid?"

"Matt shrugged. "Okay most of the time. He's kind of on my case about this class. He wants me to knock it over the wall."

"Not completely his fault. I was all over him when he was in school. I never had the chance to complete high school. I had to go to work early. I would have given my right arm for a diploma and both legs for a college degree. My family needed the help. I didn't have the luxury of school. I had to ride your dad hard. I promised myself my kids would go to school and make something of themselves with their education. Your dad wanted to goof off playing baseball. I guess I can't blame him. He was really good at the game. Baseball first and then he'd get to his studies. I had to watch him like a hawk. If I didn't, he'd sneak off."

"Seems like it's generational."

"With your dad and you, yes. You like baseball, too."

"He's pushing hard about college."

"Oh, that. What's to push? I thought you wanted a degree."

"I do, grandpa. I can push myself on that one."

"Hell, he means well. Don't sweat the small stuff. How'd the Giants do last night?"

"The transplanted "Bums" beat them 6 to 5 with come from behind bags loaded homerun."

"Crap, I hate it when Brooklyn wins."

"LA, Grandpa."

"I'm a traditionalist."

""You'll get over it, Grandpa."

"How's your Mom?"

"You know Mom. Cooking, quilting, working…"

"That's her. Your dad was lucky to find Jan. She was a real catch."

"Good cook, too."

"Especially the cookies, Kid. I really like those pretzels she dips into melted chocolate. See if she'll make some. Of course, you'll have to sneak them past the big nurse who guards this place like Fort Knox."

"I'll pass the word to her. The dough will be in the oven tonight."

"What's with your sister, Rachel?"

"Third year of college. She's the brain. Majoring in communication. I think she wants to be an elementary teacher."

"She real smart. I never had any question about that. She'll be a fine teacher."

Matt finished his breakfast, as did his grandpa. He heaped the two trays together and stowed them out of the way."

"Grandpa, what about women and minorities?"

"Kid, I take no joy in what I'm about to say. During the first two years, there were integrated camps mainly above the Mason-Dixon line. By 1935, there was none. Negroes were siphoned off to all-black camps whether in the north or south."

"Why?"

"Prejudice. Lots of it… Especially in the South… And in rural areas every where… Hell, the army was still segregated army. Jim Crow ruled below the Mason-Dixon Line. Negroes were second-class citizens."

"Is it true that Negroes were paid the same as whites?"

"Yes. The guy in the White House, or at least his wife, insisted on that. The food and housing were the same as others, too. Based on what I know, over 250,000 Negroes were in the CCC in 150 all-black camps. White officers and civilians ran the camps."

"And women?"

I heard there were a few camps, small ones for women in '33. Then they were closed. I'm only guessing, but I think people thought men needed the jobs because they were the breadwinners. Families depended on them. Anyway, between 1933 and 1941, over 3,000,000 guys were in the CCC."

"Why'd the program stop?"

"By '41, the country was gearing up for war. There were better paying jobs in the defense plants. The depression was ending and the draft was sucking up young men faster than the CCC could enlist them."

Changing the conversation, Matt's grandpa said, "Did I tell you about the book fiasco?"

"No."

"You'll love this story. But don't tell your mom. The Washington D.C. librarians wanted our guys to read. They culled through their shelves and storehouses and sent a ton of books all over America, wherever there were camps. And the guys were reading, or so it seemed. It turned out that some of the books were a bit pornographic. That's why the guys were reading, and why others were read to. It wasn't long before the books were collected and sent somewhere. More suitable books were forwarded to us."

"Anyone keep a book?"

"A few tried."

"Why did some need to be read to?"

"To answer that question, kid, I need to consult my scrapbook for some notes I stuck away. OK, here they are. You like numbers. Check this out. You'll be surprised what numbers can tell you."

Of all the CCC enlistees:

55% were from rural areas.
45% were from the cities.
3% were illiterate (40,000 were taught to read and another 110,000 took reading classes to improve).
38% had less than eight years of schooling.
48% didn't complete high school.
11% completed high school.
70% were malnourished and poorly clothed when they enlisted.

"The CCC helped a lot of people to obtain an education.

"Absolutely. A paycheck gave everyone some pride and dignity. But we had to work damn hard for the cash. Old man Roosevelt wouldn't just throw 'bucks' at us."

"You voted for him again?"

"Three more times --- '36, '40. And '44, too… I'd still vote for him if he were alive. Best damn President we've ever had."

"He has critics."

"And everyone catches a cold. Who cares? The guy saved the country and the wealthy. That's why the rich hated him. He saved their butts."

"As simple as that?"

"You got it, Kid. Hey, did I tell you about our weekends?"

"I don't so."

"One day a week, usually Saturday, we could go into town. The guys would dress up in their civilian clothes and trucks would take us to wherever there was a dance, or at least a movie or a bar for the drinkers. Guys would meet girlfriends, even a wife and kids. You had to be at a set location for a ride back at 11 p.m. otherwise you walked. Some of the big drinkers didn't always make it back on time."

"Did you ever walk, grandpa?"

"Are you kidding? Two times, as I recall."

"Grandpa, tell me about the story you wrote, the one about the forest fire."

"That's a story and a half."

Chapter 10

FOREST FIRE

JULY 1933 – CENTRAL COAST OF CALIFORNIA

The fire began on July 5, 1933, late in the afternoon in steep canyon country about twenty miles inland from the coast. As told by Matt's grandpa, and later written up by him in the CCC publication, *Youth Rebuilds*, the fire was the worst experience he ever had short of going to war. A copy of the story is in the Appendix. This is what happened.

The orders came thick and fast from the Ranger. Grab two blankets, your jacket and hat and nothing more. Get in the open pickup truck. Sit or stand, whatever you want. We're going for a ride. Forget about the blazing sun above. We've got a date with a fire.

The 1916th CCC Company of veterans was off to fight the red menace somewhere over the mountains. Taught to accept orders in wartime, they did so in peacetime.

The Ranger in charge, a tall, burly man with large hands, drove the pickup truck at breakneck speeds around the rim of a canyon and later through flatlands below. Those of us in the back were getting dizzy from all the twisting turns. Very quickly we lost all sense of direction. We could have been going to the moon for all we knew. The road was pretzel-like, winding, and twisting. We crossed the Salinas River 17 times during the long drive.

Our truck swayed back and forth as we barreled down better roads and past some very nice restaurants. We gazed at the people on the streets like vultures and they gawked back at us. Small towns slipped by and ahead of us a foreboding mountain loomed. We trembled at the thought of climbing it.

The truck kept plowing away, mile after miles, until it groaned to a stop around midnight. We could see the fire now, way off in the distance, reddish flames in the sky. We couldn't care less about the fire at that moment. We were tired, damp, and cold. All we wanted to do was sleep. We wrapped ourselves in our blankets and hit the dirt, good old "Mother Earth." We looked sort of like creatures from our prehistoric past. Of course didn't know two things at that moment. First, we were at the China Base Camp for the fire. Second, we were the greenest guys in the emerging struggle.

We slept for a few hours only to be awakened by the Ranger yelling, "All hands up." In the distance we could see the red flames spouting everywhere. Perhaps erupting would be a better word. Smoke hung over the horizon. There was fire on Black Cone Mountain. The fire was moving toward us through what is known now as the Santa Barbara National Forest.

All hands were mustered. Each of us received a tool. Some got a shovel; others were given an eight pound brush ax. As a group, we had a number of gallon jugs of water and a large bag of sandwiches, most probably two thick slices of baloney, a smear of mayo, and two slices of white bread. We packed our blankets into knapsacks and moved out.

This time there would be no trucks. We walked. We climbed. Starting out with a cool breeze, we felt pretty good. It didn't take long, however, before our feet and legs began to ache, while our shoulder cried out to lessen our backpacks. We had to climb upward over 2,000 feet along a dangerous, curving footpath. We were entirely exposed now to the sun as we pushed our way through dense brush.

By noon we were exhausted. Every drop of water was gone. Long ago we had thrown away the lunches to lighten the load. Our crew was strung out along a line a mile long. Our feet were swollen and blistered. Our legs felt like hot iron. The heat was almost unbearable.

Two things stood out in my mind. First, I was too damned tired to enjoy the beauty and majesty of the wilderness I was passing through. And second, how could I be this tired and I hadn't even gotten close to the fire?

Fortunately, at this point, the Ranger yelled out, "Pine Ridge Fire Camp below."

We now descended toward the camp closest to the fire. Former veterans as we were, we pulled ourselves together and entered the camp with a bit of dignity and a lot of bravado. We had come through country laced with almost impenetrable growth, be it the chaparral or manzanita.

After a short rest, we headed out again to build a hand line around one flank of the fire. It was ax against brush and saws against trees. With the help of others, including a large tractor, we cleared a trail almost 10-feet in width to "break the fire." In theory, the fire would slow, even stop, if it ran out of fuel. But the fire was a living thing. It needed to eat to survive. If possible, it would find a way to survive. On the other hand, we wanted to starve it.

The base of the trail was composed of decayed leaves, moss, and soil, all intertwined into fuel, however, which would burn. We had to get down on our knees to cut this stuff away. It was damned hard work. We were more fatigued than we thought possible. The boiling sun was sapping our strength. Water was scarce. We were parched. The worst things were the tiny creatures released by the fire and smoke, which attacked us without mercy ---- bugs, deerflies, and gnats. They would get in our faces, our ears, and our eyes. If we survived these monsters, there were the stinging nettles and wood ticks. So much for the joy of the great outdoors... At that moment, John Muir could have the whole forest back. With smoke in our eyes and bugs in our ears, we could have cared less. The forest was no longer a beautiful spot for a walk or a picnic. It had become a dreadful place.

Late that afternoon we stood on a granite outcropping and checked our work. The firebreak extended along a one-mile front, all up-grade. Beyond it was the fire roaring toward the line with the loudness of thunder and the severity of a hurricane. We stared in awe at the fire. The sky had turned crimson red and a wall of smoke seemed to be holding up the very heavens.

The Ranger interrupted our rapture. More lines were needed. Acting more like goats than men, we cut away brush and trees to a dry creek bed below. Our misery was reborn. We cried out for water. We were in agony. We no longer cared about the fire. "Hell, someone said, let the whole damn forest burn down." But we had taken a solemn oath to obey orders. As ex-vets, we obeyed. We carried on. We worked until twilight.

As darkness descended, we were finally ordered in. Overhead a light plane checked out the fire, surveying where it was and in what direction it was traveling. Maybe the flying Ranger also looked over our handiwork. A rumor spread that reinforcements were coming. The rumors turned out to be true.

We saw them coming toward us, 150 husky young CCC boys from camps in Santa Barbara and Monterey counties. There were boys in these camps from all over America. They checked us out as they passed. God, what a sight we were! Our faces were blackened from the ash. Our clothes looked terrible, dirty, burned in places, and not very stylish. We looked like we had been fighting a fire. We certainly smelled like we had. Christ, we looked like guys who had just refought the battle of Guadalcanal. Still, as they passed, they gave us a big hand.

The next day we worked with these youngsters. How they could work. Like demons! And they would sing and laugh like they were on a picnic.

The vets, the old guys, could hardily keep up with them. But their spirit was contagious. We picked up on it and even sang a little ourselves. In short order, we bonded with the kids, who were barely born when we answered the call in 1917.

Unaware of our new friends, the fire reached the fire-break, slowed down, and appeared to be dying out. Then it happened. An unanticipated high wind gusted into the canyon and the fire was reborn. The conflagration was coming right at us. We were on a steeply banked canyon. The fire was burning everything in its path.

We were ordered to backfire. Quickly, we poured oil on the brushes and set them afire. A friendly breeze pushed our fire toward the inferno. Once again, the fire stopped at the break waiting, I suspected, for its next attack. We hoped it wouldn't come during the night. We just wanted to rest, to sleep for a short eternity.

At night a fire should quiet down. The temperatures fall and the winds slow down. Sadly, no one told the fire. That night it burst its jail of firebreaks and charged ahead. The former flank became the new head of the fire. High winds were the culprit. They fanned the fire. Leaves, ashes, and embers were whipped through the air and over the breaks. A mass of flame jumped the lines.

Everywhere dead tired guys were awakened. That was us… We dashed to stop the new enemy. We battled the new fire along a difficult convoluted front. Again, the youngsters really proved themselves now. They had zeal, courage, and willingness that difficult to ignore. They were also reckless at times and very impetuous, almost to a fault. They just rushed into the mouth of the inferno and spit in its eye.

Though we didn't know it at the time, this was the fire's last gasp. There were now over a 1,000 people on the line and over the next three days, they fought the fire relentlessly. The fire was finally halted. The flames were subdued, but not completely out. A lot of mopping up would be necessary. The fire had burned over 7,000 acres and endangered Santa Barbara, San Luis Obispo, and Carmel before it was controlled.

The next day we headed back to Arroyo Grande, proud men who had obeyed orders and done their best, the youngsters notwithstanding. That night we would sleep the sleep of peace. An old quote accompanied me into the nocturnal world.

The forest will be gone by dawn leaving a jungle of charred stumps. Though the morning will go for some time, the yearning for that dappled shade and the notices of the creatures, who dwelt there, what comes next will be strong grasses and the mammals that graze. This is the way of life and this is what happens when lightning strikes parches undergrowth.

NIGHT FIRE FIGHTING

Chapter 11

THE DEAL

MARCH 1966 – SAN FRANCISCO

What could Matt say? He sat in awe of his grandfather and the story he had just heard. His dad had been right, Matt concluded, his grandpa was living history. He now had a better understanding of the CCC, but also the reality of young men, his own age, in the 1930's.

"Grandpa, that was quite a story."

"All true with the exception of a minor embellishment here and there."

"I'm going to include the story in my research paper. Are you okay with that?"

"Not a problem, Kid," he said with a beaming, smiling face. "Not a problem at all."

"I guess I should be going."

"Not so soon. Stay for a beer."

"You're putting me on, aren't you?"

"Yeah, I guess I am. But listen … Add this to your report. Over 3 million guys served in the CCC and when the Japanese attacked Pearl Harbor we had lots of people who were already used to military life and hard work. The Emperor didn't count on that to his everlasting unhappiness."

"I hadn't thought about that."

"Well, now you know. Another thing. Check out the preface to my copy of *Youth Rebuilds*. I've noted the pages to read."

"Thanks Grandpa."

"One last thing. Get an A+ on this report."

"You're worse than my parents."

"Right. What about the A+?"

"Guaranteed."

"That's my boy. Hey, I almost forgot. Your dad tells me you're getting a job with the Forestry Service this summer."

"He used his connections in Sacramento to get me a job with the State Division of Forestry."

"The CDF?"

"Right."

"Doing what?"

"What do you think?"

"Fire fighting?"

"Give the man a cigar."

"We can't seem to get away from fire? It must be the fate of the Samuels' family. Three generations… Think of that."

"You're counting Dad?"

"When you look down the throat of an incoming kamikaze plane, that's fire fighting."

"Grandpa, I never thought of it quite that way."

"Love yah, kid. Take care of yourself."

"Love yah, Grandpa."

As Matt headed home, his grandfather gathered together his CCC scrapbooks and wrote a note, which he attached to them. The note simply said, "For Matt Samuels. Always taste the wind. It will save your hide."

That night he passed away.

Chapter 12

LEGACY

The CCC has passed into history. It left an enduring legacy with respect to conservation, ecology, and certainly the environment. In many ways, the work of the CCC anticipated later concerns for our natural world and the magnificent heritage bestowed upon us whenever we trek on an old path in a national or state park, where once the boys of the CCC found a future. Perhaps FDR said it best on July 17, 1933 when he spoke to the CCC by radio.

You are evidence that we are seeking to get away as fast as we possibly can from soup kitchens and free rations, because the government is paying you wages and maintaining you for actual work --- work which is needed now and for the future and will bring a definite financial return to the people of the nation.

Through you the nation will graduate a fine group of strong young men, clean-living, trained to self-discipline and above all, willing and proud to work for the joy of working."

The President went on to say a few words, which the America of today should heed.

Too much in recent years large numbers of our population have sought out success as an opportunity to gain money with the least possible work.

It is time for each and every one of us to cast away self-destroying, nation-destroying efforts to get something for nothing, and to appreciate that satisfying reward and safe reward come only through honest work.

That must be the new spirit of the American future. You are the vanguard of that new spirit."

THE C.C.C. IN ACTION

MOPPING UP

PRESIDENT FRANKLIN D. ROOSEVELT

REFORESTATION

Fireside Chat – May 7, 1933 – FDR Addresses the Nation

We are giving the opportunity of employment to one-quarter of a million of the unemployed, especially the young men who have dependents, to go into forestry and flood prevention work. In creating the Civilian Conservation Corps, we are killing two birds with one stone. We are clearly enhancing the value of our natural resources and second, we are relieving an appreciable amount of actual distress.

Accomplishments

The CCC lasted nine years, enrolling more than 3,000,000 men building recreational facilities, especially trails, park shelters, campgrounds and scenic vistas. The work of the CCC can be seen today in national parks and national forests and in the thousands of culverts they installed to prevent land erosion. But most of all, it gave hope to millions of young men that things would get better.

FDR AND C.C.C. RECRUITS

Part III

THE BOYS OF CRESCENT CITY

Chapter 13

SUMMER JOB

JUNE 1966 – SAN FRANCISCO

It's a college tradition. Unless your parents are very affluent, most college students seek out temporary summer work to help pay for next year's tuition costs. At times this can be a challenging endeavor, since thousands of collegians are thrown into the job market at about the same time. In such circumstances, it's always nice to know someone who can juice your way, get a good word in for you, or simply let you know about a job opening before the general publics is aware of it. One could argue, this isn't fair, but what is in our competitive world? Juice is important and not just at the breakfast table. What you know counts. Who you know can count even more.

In the case of Matt Samuels, this was certainly the case. Thanks to his father, a peerless reporter for the *San Francisco Chronicle*, Matt got a great job with the California Division of Forestry (CDF). His dad had connections in Sacramento with folks who owed him a little something for past favors: news stories covered in a fair and objective manner, names mentioned, things said or not said, little things (or favors) that make the world go around. It was nice having a professional journalist for a father with an "in."

The spring semester of high school had come and gone for Matt. Overall, it was a success. He had played ball and done okay as a pitcher against improved competition in his league. His school classes had been a "walk." Only in statistics had he pushed the homework lamp. As to his college course, he took to the US History class with zest and wrote his research paper on the CCC with zeal and great sadness.

His "grandpa" was gone and Matt missed him terribly.

Grandpa was buried in a military cemetery just south of San Francisco, a place called San Bruno. Grandpa's friends and family had gathered three months ago to say "goodbye." It had been a cold morning with a brisk breeze blowing through the well-maintained forest of headstones. The sunlight was struggling to break through the light fog hovering over the Bay Area.

The VFW conducted the services, more secular than sectarian. Friends and family were asked to say a few words. Matt's father had reminded everyone that his dad had lived a full life through troubled times in our nation's history, most prominently the First World War, the Great Depression, and WWII. But he was a tough old guy who somehow found a way to survive. He had done his best, which is all anyone can ask.

After Jan and Rachel said their words, it was Matt's turn. Though it was difficult, he swiped away tears and said all that mattered.

"Grandpa, I'm going to get that "A+."

At the conclusion of the service, Matt's dad was handed a Bible and an American flag. Then a bugler played taps in a final tribute. The sounds floated over the gathering and across the mystic divide between life and death. As in a Hollywood movie, sunlight finally burst through the thinning fog to embrace the Samuels family and their loss.

Two months later, plus a few days, Matt got his "A+."

The following day, he drove out to San Bruno and to the gravesite where his grandpa was buried. Standing before the headstone, Matt read his entire research paper to his grandpa. It was an honor for him to do so.

A month later he ventured forth to meet his destiny, to confront the fire, which was always lurking out there smoldering before it animated itself to challenge all young men.

"Are you sure you have everything?" Matt's mother asked. "Once you're on the bus, it's too late to think about what you left behind."

"I've got everything, Mom."

The family was standing in the waiting room of the old Greyhound Bus Station at Seventh and Market across the street from the Rincon Annex, the major downtown Post Office in San Francisco. The station was quite something. It was the terminal for at least many buses and destinations. Sixty long lines of buses parked at an angle in their stalls defined the place. Next to each bus stop were travelers lining up to board after other folks disembarked. It was a busy place, night and day, when people were willing to let "Greyhound do the driving."

"I need to get in line," Matt said with impatient glee. "Got to go."

"Write to us," his mom urged him. "Not just a postcard."

"Don't fall in love with one of those woodsy girls," Rachel prompted with a big smile."

"No chance, Rachel."

"Keep your cool," his dad reminded him no matter what."

"Got it, Dad."

With that, Matt grabbed his duffel bag and hurried to catch his bus. As he did, his mom said, "Oh, he's so young to be leaving us."

"Don't fret, Jan. He'll be fine."

Robert Samuels was sure Matt would be OK. They had talked about the summer job before the boy left.

"A few things, Matt."

"Only a few?"

"Hopefully for both our sakes."

"Okay."

"No matter how bad the food is at the station, eat it. If you're on a fire, it might be the last chance to dine for awhile."

"How bad is bad, dad?"

"Just eat. And get your sleep. Once you're on the line, sleep is a forgotten word."

"That I can do," he said with a big smirk. "Like Mom and Rachel, I love to sleep."

"You do at that."

"Unlike some people…"

"Let's not get personal."

"Me, get personal. Never."

They both laughed at that. Then his father got real serious.

"Matt, you've been lucky. You grew up in a fairly liberal city where anti-Semitism is diminished compared to some places, including small towns. More than likely, you'll be stationed in a small town. You'll hear things about Jews. Some of the comments will be mean spirited. Try not to let them get to you."

"I'm always cool, dad."

"Keep it that way. Another thing… You're a political appointee. You're taking the place of another boy from the area where you'll be working. Some of the guys in the station won't like that. They might want to take out their feelings…"

"By fighting?"

"Yes."

"I won't."

"Good. You don't want to lose your job."

"Gotcha."

"One last thing."

"Really? Matt asked in a teasing way.

"Always taste the wind."

"That's what grandpa told me."

"You're grandfather taught me the same thing. When you're on the fire line, two things are really important. First, do you have a way out if the fire changes direction? Second, feel the wind. Let it slide over you. Listen to it. Taste it. It's a living thing, and it speaks."

"Dad..."

"Hear me out. When the wind talks, pay attention to it. It's the great ally of fire. Much like a charioteer, it drives the fire, directs the fire. It is the other side of fire, its shadow, if you will. If you understand the wind, you'll be safe."

Matt realized this was serious stuff his father was talking about. He also realized his father was trying to protect him.

"I'll taste the wind."

The bus ride northward was an ordeal. The Greyhound Bus left the terminal at 5:15 p.m. sharp, turned sharply on Mission and headed west to Van Ness, where it joined traffic headed for the Golden Gate Bridge and Marin County and its "milk run" up the Coast along Highway 101. The big bus rumbled and screeched to a stop in every town on the map, or so it seemed to Matt --- Santa Rosa, Lake Port, Willits, Leggett, Garberville, and finally, Fortuna.

The ride had been an ordeal for Matt. The bus itself was okay. The seats were big and roomy, and very comfortable. The older lady sitting next to him was friendly and not too inquisitive. She slept a lot. She was going to Portland to visit her daughter and grandchildren. No, Matt's ordeal had quite a different source. He was deathly afraid he would miss his stop. His work orders required him to be in Fortuna and to report to the CDF Headquarters just south of the town. After stowing his duffle bag under the bus in a large compartment for suitcases and cardboard boxes, he had talked to the driver.

"I need to get off at the CDF HQ before town. Can you drop me there along the highway?"

"Sure."

To stay awake, Matt forced himself to think about next fall, when he would attend college. He was going to Cal, just across the Bay in Berkley, where a history major awaited him and probably a teaching credential. He always enjoyed the subject and thought he got along well with the younger set, especially the sophomores he tutored in high school for a few bucks. He would minor in business just in case the classroom proved not to his liking. What was it his grandpa said in passing? "Always have a backup plan."

The hours drifted by slowly. Matt's thoughts were constantly interrupted by a nightmarish thought. What if the driver didn't remember? What would happen if he slept all the way to Portland? How would he get back to California? How would he explain things in Fortuna? He fought the need to fall asleep. That proved to be impossible. Try as he might, he finally fell into the hands of an uneasy sleep. He dreamed of missing his stop, again and again.

Suddenly, he was fully awake. He felt a disquieting feeling. Something was wrong. The bus was very quiet except for the chorus of snoring and deep breathing. But something wasn't right. Then he had it. He couldn't hear the wind pushing against the bus as it flew down the highway. The bus wasn't moving. The engine was idling. Oh, my God, he thought, have we reached Portland? Why didn't the bus driver stop in Fortuna?

Matt realized someone was gently touching him, shaking his shoulders. Fearfully, he looked up and stared at the bus driver, who had a big smile on his face that shone through his late hour beard.

"We're here, kid."
"Already?"
"You've been asleep for hours. Time to go."

The driver had pulled over along 101 just across the highway from the CDF HQ. It was 5:30 a.m. in the morning. It was time to grab his duffle bag and face his future.

Chapter 14

CRESCENT CITY STATION

JUNE 1966 – HUMBOLDT AND DEL NORTE COUNTIES

Slinging his duffle bag over his shoulder, Matt crossed the wide, four-lane highway and sat down in front of the Main Office of the CDF for the two most northern counties along the coast, Humboldt and Del Norte. He felt miserable. He was cold and tired, and the Office didn't open until 7:30 a.m. It was only 6:00 a.m. He tried to take his mind off his troubles. He concentrated on the items in his duffle bag.

As required by the CDF, Matt had brought a sleeping bag, three tan, long-sleeved shirts, two pair of Levi pants, an Eisenhower Levi jacket, six pairs of heavy white woolen socks, a pair of strong work gloves, assorted briefs and undershirts compliments of *Fruit of the Loom*, and a pair of tough working boots. Besides all this, and at the request of his City College professor, Matt brought with him Winston Churchill's five-book collection on World War II. He was trying to remember the items in his toiletry bag, when the Office door opened.

An older guy came out, lit up a cigarette, and then noticed Matt sitting forlornly on the porch. For a few seconds, they just stared at each other. The old guy had a cook's hat on, something like Lincoln's top hat, only white. He wore a long white apron, which long ago had stopped being very white. His pants were checkered, blue lines running against each other. A three-quarters smoked cigarette rested precariously in his mouth. What Matt looked like to the other man was beyond his ability to speculate.

"Who are you?" the cook asked.
"Matt."
"Lost your last name?"
"Samuels."
"Where are you from?"
"The city."
"Does it have a name?"
"San Francisco."
"Oh, you're the one."
"What?"
"The appointee."

The old man made the word sound like a disease. Matt wondered what he had gotten into.

"I guess I am."
"No guessing involved."
"I needed a job."
"Don't we all."

"I guess I'm early. The bus driver let me off a few minutes ago."

"I saw that. You're not the first kid who has crossed the highway. You won't be the last. Well, come on in. You look half-frozen. What you need is a hot cup of coffee."

Matt followed the cook into the office, down a hall and into the base kitchen where two guys were working. They were about Matt's age.

"Meet Matt," the cook said flatly. "He's from the city, the big one with the bridges."

The two guys gave Matt the "once over," tough looks to engender fear and intimidation.

"Hi," Matt said in his most controlled fashion. "What are you doing?"
"K.P. duty, city guy."

There it was again, Matt thought. His dad had been right. He'd have to work hard to stay out of trouble with these country boys.

"Here's your coffee, black, no sugar, no cream. No girly stuff in it. The way a man should drink his Java."
"Thanks."

Matt tried the coffee. It was hot and had quite a kick to it, sort of like trying your first cigarette or hard booze. He couldn't help it. His face contorted for a moment as it adjusted to the alien liquid flowing into his body. The cook laughed and said, "You'll get used to it kid."

"What do I call you, sir?" Matt asked.
"Sir… I like that. Kid has manners. Call me Biscuits."
"Biscuits?"
"You hard of hearing, kid?"
"No, sir."
"Good. And by the way, welcome to the CDF, the finest firefighting force in this man's forest. While you're waiting to be processed, you can help these guys out."

For the next thirty minutes, Matt got a taste of KP duty: setting a table for ten people, washing and drying pots, and mopping up some spills in the dining room. Somehow it didn't feel like firefighting. Where was the adventure? The romance?

Soon the other guys filed in for breakfast, mostly high school and college age guys. Also with them were his bosses, the Captain, the

Foreman, and the chief mechanic. To one and all he was introduced as the "guy from San Francisco." That met with blank looks and a shrugging of shoulders.

Matt's welcome included processing his papers: tax withholding forms, Social Security forms, health insurance forms, everything, it seemed, except for the racing form. There was some concern when it was discovered he had spent one night in juvenile hall for assault and battery.

"What about this?" the female, civilian secretary asked. "You did jail time?"

"Three nights. Juvenile Hall."

"Who'd you hit""

"It's a long story."

"Give me the shortened version."

"My high school buddies were attacked by some jerks in North Beach, who were drunk. We fought back. I got in a few good licks. When the police came, I didn't run. My buddies took off. I was arrested."

"For?"

"Assault and battery."

"You were a minor?"

"Yes."

"Go to court?"

"Yes."

"And?"

"I was a first time offender. I got probation."

"That's it?"

"That's it."

Apparently Matt's explanation was sufficient. An hour later, he found himself riding on the back of a CDF pumper truck, along with boxes of food supplies. In the front, his new immediate boss, Doug, was driving. Seated next to him was Biscuits. As he threw his duffle bag onto the truck and climbed in himself, he asked, "Where are we going?"

"Crescent City, Killer," the cook yelled.

The slightly more than 100 mile trip along Highway 101 took three hours. Matt passed through new towns, which in time became familiar to him since they had CDF stations --- Bridgeville, Trinidad, Klamath, Arcata, and finally Crescent City. The ride up the Coast was bone chilling. Seated outside the cab and a target for the blustery wind off the ocean, he got his first taste of really cold weather. Two hours later, the truck arrived at the CDF station, which was just north of the town along 101 and next to a company that provided natural gas to its customers. As the pumper drove into the station Matt checked out what would eventually be his home for five fire seasons.

The first thing he noticed was the water tower. It supplied water not only to the station, but also for the station's pumper truck, which held 250 gallons. Nearby was an old-fashioned gas pump used to fill the truck's 60-gallon thirsty gas tank. He saw a long table-like structure with slats every six inches. It looked sort of like a ladder resting parallel to the ground. It was about 300-feet in length. On top of it was a 2-inch cotton hose, which was being scrubbed and cleaned by two fellows, who didn't seem to take kindly to the job. Where the truck had stopped was a four-truck garage. As he would later learn, the garage could hold two trucks, a jeep, and a small "cat," such as a "D-4" tractor. Not far from the garage was the barracks building, a squat white structure that housed the mess hall and kitchen.

"Off the truck, Samuels," Doug yelled. We're here. Biscuits will show you where to put your stuff."

The interior of the barracks was basic to armies all over the world. There was a row of eight cots on either side of the room. A small bureau was next to each cot with a tired reading lamp on each one. At the front and back of the sleeping quarters was a line of wooden lockers with air vents --- holes --- drilled into them. They were about six feet in height and could hold a lot of personal stuff. In the middle of the room there was a large table and six chairs. In an adjacent room were the showers and the indoor latrine. Three large windows on either side of the larger room permitted sunlight to filter in through old curtains.

"Unpack," Biscuits said. "You have bed and locker number 7. Hope it's a lucky number for you."

"Me, too," Matt said with hope in his heart. "Me, too."

It took Matt a few minutes to square away his things. That was good because a bell sounded and other new recruits came into the barracks from all over. It was time for their mid-morning coffee break. Joining the guys was the truck driver, the foreman, and the cook. They gathered around the large table, where the Foreman said, "It's time for you guys to meet our newest member. The guy we told you about from Frisco."

Frank was the boss, the Foreman --- the man in charge of us, the summer workers, here in the station and out on the fire line. He was a full timer, a professional firefighter. He spoke and we obeyed. He was God.

He was a tall man, a little over six feet and about 35-years in age. He was married and lived in Crescent City when off duty. He was a redhead with very light skin and a bucketful of freckles. Matt soon learned these things about his boss. First, he was always right, even when he was wrong. Second, he really didn't like college kids or anyone really into books. Third, he cared little for political appointees. Fourth, he hated to lose in cards, especially where hard cash was on the table. If you played poker with him, you needed to lose. If you won, God help you. Fifth, he didn't like people who were taller than he was.

To Matt's way of thinking, he was on Frank's S-list before the fire season even began. He was a college kid with a bucket load of Winston Churchill's books stored in his locker. He was a political appointee. No way around that one. He was competitive and didn't like to lose. That didn't bid well for playing cards. And lastly, at almost 6 foot, 5 inches, he was taller than Frank. Not much he could do about that beyond walking with a slouch when near his boss. Matt wondered how all this might turn out. He would try to remain optimistic.

Frank did have some saving graces. He was competent. He was cautious. He was careful. All of these characteristics served him well --- and his crew --- when dealing with a fire gone wild. Where he might bluster and lose control in a card game, it was the model of calmness in the field. Matt figured it was a good trade-off to have a boss who kept his cool under fire.

The truck driver was Doug, a young man in his mid-twenties, At about 275 pounds, he looked like an offensive lineman, big and strong. Most of it was muscle, though no one would ever accuse him of missing a meal. He was a jovial, meaty guy with a good sense of humor, and a cigarette constantly dangling from his lips. A cherished *Zippo* lighter seemed to be his best friend beyond his new wife and baby girl. His family lived a few miles north at Smith River.

Doug could handle a truck, jeep, or tractor. He probably could drive anything that had wheels. He was in charge of all the necessary paper work, which the Foreman detested. The forms demanded by the CDF seemed endless. Matt became Doug's best friend in time when the truck driver learned the kid from San Francisco could type and didn't mind filling out the multi-page fire report forms. And why should Matt mind? This was better than scrubbing endless feet of cotton hose.

One of the summer workers was Johnny Youngblood, a full-blooded Yurok Indian, who came to like Matt. Johnny was short, stout, and strong Usually he was on the silent side. For some reason, he decided to become a close friend of Matt, even to the point of taking the city kid fishing in the mouth of the Klamath River to catch large salmon swimming upstream to lay their eggs and die. Matt would never forget that day. The boats, bulging with fisherman, were so close you could have walked across the river and never gotten wet. Though he had a few tugs on his line, Matt never caught anything. Johnny's luck was better, or his skill. He caught three salmon.

Another summer worker was James Molina who liked to be called "Jim." He was a local guy from Ferndale, a small town just south and west of Fortuna, where Victorian style homes were prominent. Jim was attending Humboldt State College. He was in his second year with a biology/forestry combination major. He wanted to make the CDF a career. At about 5'7", he was shorter than Matt and a little pudgy. He had to wear glasses, which gave him a studious appearance, even when he was working the fire line. He was also congenial and glad to help a new guy like Matt.

There's always a tough guy in any summer group in the CDF, or at least a guy who thinks he can take anyone. And there's always an older guy, who looked out of place with high school and college age fellows. The tough guy was Mike Henderson. He was from Eureka, the biggest city along the coast in Humboldt County. Mike was getting ready to join the Army at the end of the summer. Over time, Matt got the distinct perception that Mike wanted to fight him. He was always making rude remarks, stupid punk stuff, which, though harmless, could get on your nerves after awhile. Matt tried to stay away from this guy.

The old man was Larry. He was from Clovis and nearly 50-years old. For Matt, five decades equaled half a century and "old." Larry had been in the CCC for two years. Now he was the chief mechanic. He enjoyed talking to Matt about his days at a CCC camp in Montana. Matt enjoyed his company. They, it turned out, shared a common interest.

There were five others, of course, who worked at the station. As a group, all the guys had a few things in common. Everyone smoked, mostly *Lucky Strike* and *Camels*. Matt gave in to peer pressure and smoked a *Kool* cigarette now and then. He didn't like the smoke, but the menthol felt good in his throat, especially on the fire line, when his throat was parched from the heat and smoke. That and he also liked "Willie the Penguin." Everyone drank coffee, hot and black, and lit up while doing so. Gambling on payday was a favorite of most, though Matt learned quickly to avoid this sin. Few read the daily paper, and just about everyone checked out the latest *Gent* and *Playboy* magazines. Large breasts demanded their literary attention. Here Matt admitted, he fell to temptation. How could he avoid doing so? The magazines were everywhere except when the boss' wife visited or any female for that matter. Then, magically all such material was replaced with *Life Magazine* and the *Readers Digest*. In such moments, the crew might be mistaken for a choir group from the local Catholic Church.

These were the guys Matt came to know and, for the most part, to like. He would spend considerable time with them. In the meantime, he had a lot to learn about fire fighting. With that in mind, he was glad to hear Doug say, "Tomorrow is a school day, guys. You're going to learn about fire and how to fight it."

TYPICAL 1950'S PUMPER TRUCK

Chapter 15

LESSONS

JUNE 1966 – CRESCENT CITY

The next day the crew gathered in the large garage. Here Frank was holding court.

"I'm going to talk to you about tools, then fire strategy, and then about the town. Any questions before I start."

There were no questions. Frank picked up a tool I had never seen before. "This is a great tool. It's called a McLeod. One side is a hoe, which easily lets you scrap a fire line. The other side has a broad-tooth rake that can pull away duff and raw earth. Malcolm McLeod created this in 1905. He was a US Forest Service Ranger. You'll be practicing with it later. When you do, I only want to see your butts and the teeth facing downward when you're carrying it. You'll be bent over putting in a mock fire trail. Any questions?"

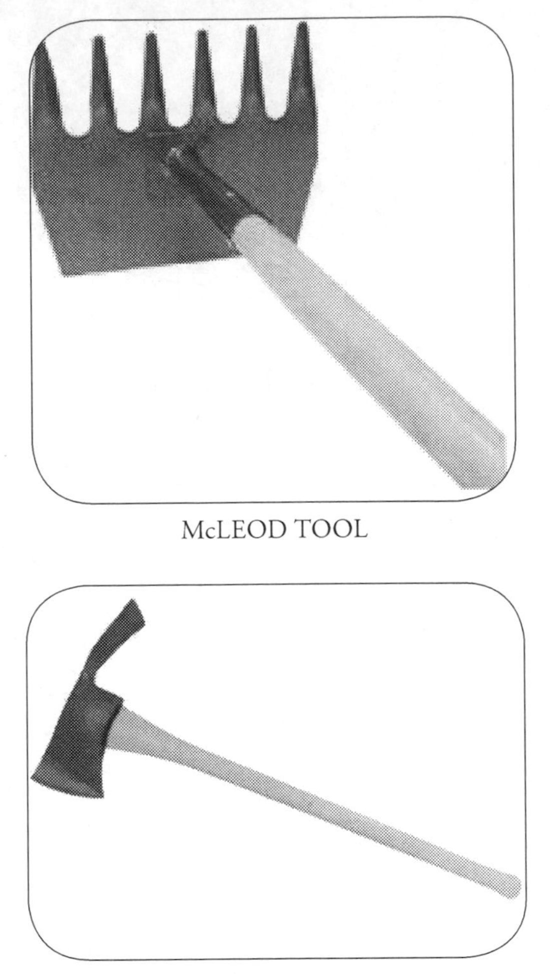

McLEOD TOOL

PULASKI TOOL

There were no questions.

"This is a Pulaski. One end is a tough hoe or adze. The other end is an ax. It's a great tool for constructing a firebreak. You can drag and cut with this tool. It really cuts into the dirt. But be careful with it. It's heavy and sharp. You can hurt someone or yourself if you don't use it correctly. Ed Pulaski invented this tool in 1911. He was also a member of the US Forestry Service. You'll practice with this tool later. And when you do, be careful. It's not a baseball bat. You can kill someone with it. Any questions?"

Hearing nothing, Frank went on. This is a portable McCulloch water pump. When we go in on a lightning strike, we sometimes take this if there is a source of water. It's heavy and difficult to carry. I'll show you. Samuels come here."

Matt heard his name and stepped forward nervously. Frank turned him around and then strapped the portable pump on his back. He pulled the shoulder straps tight.

"How does that feel?"

"OK, I guess."

"Well, let's find out. Trot down to the end of the grounds, about 150 yards and then return, still at a trot. Got it?"

"Yes."

"Try 10-4. It means the same thing."

Matt took off at a trot. Within seconds the straps were biting into his shoulders and his back was starting to ache from the constant banging of the pump against it. This tool, he though, was a real pain in the ass. He reached the end of the grounds and trotted back.

"How was it?" Frank asked.

"No picnic."

"Right. Now think about carrying this monster in the dark with rain falling on you as you move uphill through dense forage to find the lightning strike."

Matt didn't want to think about it.

Doug pulled the pump off Matt and then brought over a coil of cotton hose. "This is another tool, two inch cotton hose to connect to the McCulloch. The coil weighs about seventy pounds. I need a volunteer. Thanks, Samuels. It's good to see you're not afraid to try anything."

Matt was beginning to see the writing on the wall. They were testing the city boy. Would he crack? Could he handle the pressure?

Doug handed the coil to Matt. "Just hold it like a baby. Don't drop it or let any sharp edge cut it. It's not worth a damn with holes in it. OK, just trot the way you did before."

MCCULLOCH PUMP

COTTON HOSE

Some baby, Matt thought as he trotted. It's heavy and awkward. He couldn't imagine climbing uphill with it unless it could be strapped to his back. As for the test, he was determined to beat these guys. Fortunately, the baseball and football practices the coaches put him through stood by him at this moment. Though he was hurting, he didn't let on as he finished his run.

"How was that, Doug asked, a shy smile on his face."

"10-4."

"Which do you prefer, the pump or the hose?"

"The McCulloch."

"It's your baby, then."

Of course, Matt wasn't sure he had made the right decision, pump or hose. That would only be determined on a fire.

Frank interrupted Matt's musings, saying, "A word about the hose; one of the first things we do after a fire call is to wash and dry the cotton hose, and, if necessary, make repairs. We all join in on this. That's why the rack. We stretch the hose out, inspect it for tears, and then wash it. After drying we recoil it and store it on the pumper. A second coil is already stored in case of an emergency. Got it?"

THE HOSE RACK

Later Matt would learn how to work the pump and how to keep the filter clear. He learned about water pressure and the limits of cotton hose. He learned he could carry it uphill no matter what his back and legs said to the contrary.

"Listen up. This is a tool, too." Frank was pointing to the pumper truck. "This Dodge has a V-8 in her and 400 horse power. She's 4-wheeled. She can go almost any place a mule can travel. She carries 250 gallons of water and almost 60 gallons of gas. The hose wheel holds 150 yards of tough rubber hose. This is supplemented by 400-yards of cotton hose. Two men in the front, six guys on the open back. She carries our tools, food, and drinking water. She carries our sleeping bags. She's our best friend. In a pinch, the winch in the front can pull her up a hill, or help us pull down a snag. We've got a two-way all- channel radio in the cab. It keeps us up to date on what's happening. You will take care of this tool. Each day you will check to see that she is clean, highly polished, fueled, and loaded with water. When we come back from a fire, she'll be fully, and I repeat this, she'll be fully checked out and cleaned in case we catch a call. That happens before we shower or eat, or take a piss. Any questions?"

If there were questions, no one asked one.

"Another thing… We work with an even bigger tool. We work with the "big cats," the tractors with 8-foot blades. The people who drive them are called "cat-skinners." They're an unruly group. They smoke a lot. They drink a lot. They curse a lot. And we can't do without them. They take their D-8 and D-9 cats right up to the fire. They knock down stuff in their way. They carve up the land and put a great firebreak in much faster than our hand tools. When you see a "cat," respect its power. Don't get in its way. It doesn't hate you, but it will crush you if it hits you. It can be a mechanical monster. The threads are made of steel. They bite into anything they roll over. When you hear the diesel engine, or the threads cranking, get the hell out of the way. When you see a cat-skinner, show some respect. It's not easy driving one of these babies, especially at night as they crawl along a steep embankment or move downhill into a gulch. Sitting in the cab of a "big D" is no joke. Any questions?

"Do we ever get to ride on one? Matt asked.

"Only if the cat-skinner lets you. And you better have a good reason."

"Like what?"

"Starting a backfire with phosphorous grenade."

"Sounds cool."

"You think so, Samuels? How about I put you down for the first chance we get?"

"10-4, sir."

Frank had to admire the kid. Maybe he was all bluff. Time would tell.

"OK Ladies, Frank said sarcastically. It's time to learn about fire. Doug you take over."

"A fire is a living thing. It begins as a tiny spark, then it feeds and grows, aided by a fuel source and variable currents of air. It has a constant need for fuel, oxygen, and heat. Perfect fire conditions always include low humidity and high, blustering gusts of wind. Fire is a kind of shape-shifting monster. It can appear to die, then find itself reborn. It can change direction on a dime. Yesterday's flank can become today's point. When it's out of control, it can crown, burning across the tops of giant trees at a speed faster than our rig. It can explode and throw sparks miles. It cares little for our presence. And, if it can, it will burn our homes, towns, and even our loved ones. It is not to be trifled with. Never. Always respect fire."

Doug didn't finish with the usual, "Are there any questions?" He just turned the show back over to Frank.

"Let's talk about fire strategy. If we're the first truck to a grass fire, we douse the edges with water. We work the flanks. We almost never attack from the front, the blistering head of the fire. We put in an additional hand line if we suspect there are hot spots in the burned out area. Again, we never get in front of a fast moving grass fire. Again, I emphasize this; we attack it from the flanks, squeezing the fire as we move toward the point. If the fire is in a wooded area, it's the same deal. Attack from the flanks and throw a line around it as quickly as possible. That means clearing our thickets of brush and saplings, or high branches that could carry the fire across the line. If the fire is too hot, or jumps the line and threatens to blow, we can always backfire and that's dangerous. This calls for three things: first, you have favorable winds to blow the new fire back into the old one. Second, you have a good line in case the backfire doesn't work. Third, you have an escape route so you won't be trapped. That's the most important thing. Wherever we go, we've got to have an escape route."

Matt heard the last line in Frank's talk. His grandpa had also reminded him of this. His dad had mentioned it, too.

Matt took heed.

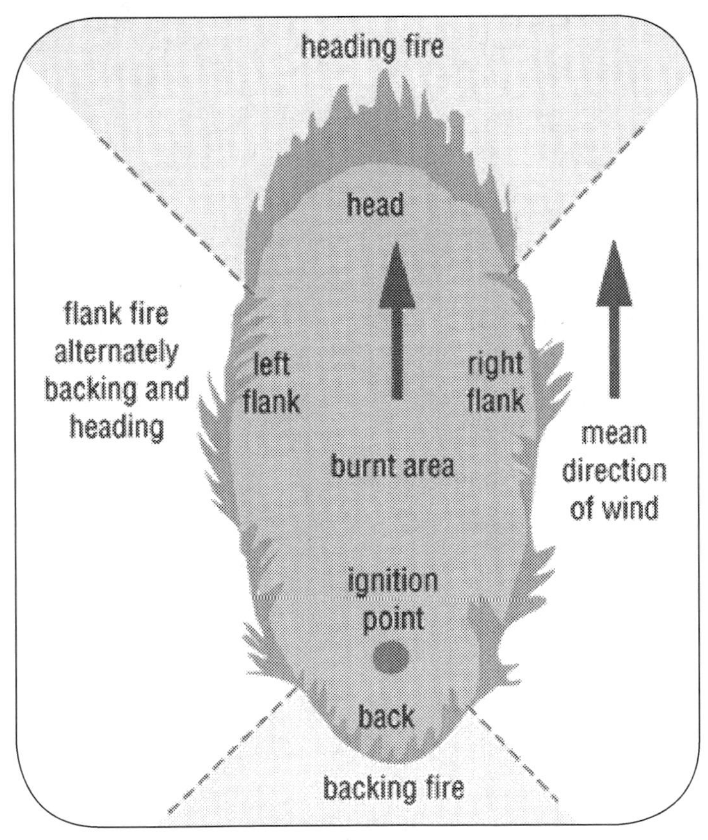

DIAGRAM OF A FOREST FIRE

Chapter 16

LETTERS HOME

JULY 1966 – CRESCENT CITY

A month had gone by and Matt was getting used to the CDF routine. He got up at 6:00 a.m. to the blare of Frank's voice and the suddenly turned on bright lights of the barracks. "Up and at them …" Frank's final word to complete the sentence bordered on the sexual, the crude, and certainly uncomplimentary descriptions of the human anatomy. In some ways, Frank's colorful descriptions of his workers reminded Matt of his old football coach. The two men seemed cut from the same piece of cloth.

They went to bed at 10:00 p.m. when the barrack lights clicked off. That was okay. After a full day of physical work, sleep came easily. Breakfast was served at 7:00 a.m. sharp, and not later. Lunch was at noon. Dinner was served at 5:00 p.m. Two fifteen-minute coffee breaks were permitted, one at 10 a.m., the other at 3 p.m. At all other times, you were working on something. A full list of projects was posted each day. You found your name and hustled to complete your job. Life was orderly, since the clock and the posted assignments controlled everything. And in the background, there was always Frank and Doug, chain smoking and yelling out orders, or tenderly offering suggestion, such as "Get your ass in gear."

Only one thing could disrupt this well organized and highly oiled regimen. If the P.A. went off in the yard, it usually meant only one thing: a fire call had come in and the station was slated to respond. It was a little like hearing, "Pilots, man your planes." Within one minute, the guys stopped what they were doing, grabbed what they needed, and hustled to the pumper truck and jeep. They buttoned their Levi jackets and hitched the strap of their World War I styled aluminum helmets to keep them from flying off as the pumper truck hit the main road, siren screaming and lights flashing. Frank pushed and practiced this one-minute drill. If you didn't make it on time, you could count on lots of hose cleaning.

Days off were staggered to always maintain a nearly full crew. The guys generally went home. Matt, on the other hand, stayed around the station or walked the two miles into Crescent City. Frequently, he got around by hitching rides. If a fire call came while he was off duty but in the station, he went with the guys.

By the middle of July, Matt decided to write a longer letter to his folks to sort of summarize things to that point.

Dear Mom and Dad, and Rachel,

I hope everything is OK with you. Things are fine here. I'm feeling fine, eating well, and growing muscles due to the daily physical work. So mom, there's no need to fret. I'm just fine. Believe it or not, I wash my clothes once a week and even take an iron to them. You need to be stylish in the CDF.

I wish I could tell you we've been on lots of fires. That just hasn't happened. The weather has been on the cooler side and a bit wet, so maybe that's the reason for the few alarms. The prediction for August is for high temperatures, very low humidity, and chaotic winds. That's the perfect combination for a good fire. I hate to admit it, but I'm looking forward to some action. I wouldn't want the summer to end without at least one good adventure.

I've learned a lot about fire fighting equipment and strategies to use in dealing with a fire. I seem to have a knack for this sort of thing.

Dad, I've decided to take you up on your offer. If the deal is still on, I'll send you as much of my paycheck as possible and you'll match whatever I save. This seems like a winner for me, so thanks in advance.

Now a confession… No, I haven't fallen in love. No, I didn't lose my job. No, I didn't get into a fight. No, it was something far worse. I went snipe hunting.

The guys really tricked me. I can't believe I fell for their ruse. It began this way. New CDF guys had to be initiated by looking for and catching a snipe, which is actually a bird found along the seashore. But, I should add, not in the woods. I was given a burlap bag and a flashlight on a moonless night and told to look for the snipe. The guys taught me some snipe calls so I was ready to catch one. I had three hours in which to find one. Alone in the woods near our station, I hunted for the evasive snipe. As you can guess, I didn't bag a snipe. I came back to the station where the guys were waiting with hoots and laughs at my expense.. They had really fooled me. They sure knew how to make fun of a credulous newcomer from the city. What a practical joke! I can't wait to try it on someone.

I want to share two more stories with you. The first concerns a deer. The second is about KP duty.

A few days ago, a State Highway Officer drove into the station with a deer tied to his vehicle. Apparently, it had been hit by a tourist and killed. Fortunately for us, the deer wasn't too mangled by the collision. Our cook, Biscuits, accepted the deer. Since we're on a tight per meal budget, any deer venison would reduce our costs, and permit us to buy extra items like ice cream.

The very next day I was called to the Office. My boss, Frank, who is the Foreman, wanted me to skin the deer. Naturally, I explained I was slightly inexperienced in this area. He said Biscuits, our cook, and the other guys would be there to assist me. What could I do? My pride was at stake.

In the yard as we call the station grounds, the deer had been hung up on a pole, upside down, belly facing outward. The cook was standing there with three big pots and one heck of a butcher knife. The thing looked like a bayonet. I was told to cut the poor animal from the anus downward to the stomach and to the throat. The thought of doing this was repulsive. I realized then that I would have died on the frontier without a supermarket close by. I also understood that all the guys were watching me. Hell, I thought, when in Crescent City, do what the natives want.

I made the incision, the anus to throat, clear down the belly. Then two things happened in rapid succession. First, the deer's entrails, its guts, now freed, poured out, blood and all. Second, the smell hit me. Whack. With regret, I tell you your faithful son passed out, right then and there. I was brought back to life by a bucket of cold water. Mercifully, the cook took over while the guys had a good laugh, once more at my expense. I would rather have been snipe hunting.

All of us have KP duty for a week. It means getting up earlier than everyone except the cook, and finishing your day later than others. Your duties include setting the table for all meals, cleaning the "heads," and helping the cook with his chores. That includes sweeping and mopping the mess hall, bathroom, and kitchen. It's a long day, pretty much without a break. You have KP duty for five straight days.

On one occasion, Biscuits left to order supplies in town. He told me to clean the kitchen. He wanted a spotless floor, stove, tables, and cooking utensils. He gave me three hours to get the job done. Apparently, a "big-wig" was coming in from Fortuna to check out our station.

He left and I went to work. Mom, you would have been so proud of me. I cleaned, swept, polished, and dusted. Nothing escaped my KP eyes. I was a whirling dervish in action. Mr. Clean had nothing on me. When Biscuits returned, I was ready for his review.

He checked everything and muttered out loud, "Seems OK." At other times, he said, "Nice job, kid." I was soaking in the compliments. I didn't realize I was being set up.

At our old-fashioned wrought iron stove, which was big enough to cook for the entire Diamond Heights neighborhood, Biscuits paused, bent down almost flat to the ground, and looked under the stove. He extended a hand and brought out some eggshells. "What's this?" he said with alarm.

"Eggshells?"

"Very observant."

"Where'd they come from?" I asked desperately. "I know I swept and mopped under the stove."

"Well, you sure missed these," Biscuits countered as he cracked the shells in an outraged hand. The shells sounded like cannons going off.

"I don't know what to say," I said imploringly. "Is this the end of my career in the CDF?"

Biscuits just stared at me, darts flying from his eyes. Then slowly a slight mile emerged that led to a hearty chuckle. "My boy, you've been had. I just palmed these shells and pretended to find them."

I had to laugh. What else could I do?

I had some other misadventures. I tried fishing. I spent one day fishing along a quiet creek not far from the CDF Station. Using a borrowed line and lures I went forth. To my utter surprise, I actually caught fifteen fish, each about six inches long. Proudly, I brought them back to Biscuits. As I recall:

"Nice catch, Matt."

"Thanks."

"What are you going to do with them?"

"Can be have them for dinner?"

"Sure. Of course, you'll have to clean them and get the scales off. Then I'll show you how to cook them."

"Take off the scales?"

You get the picture. I did it. That, however, took some of the fun out of fishing.

One last story… Everyday our bed was inspected. The bed had to be tight, military style. Frank would take a fifty-cent piece and flip it on the bed. If it bounced just right, the bed was made just right. If not, he's tear the bed down and bellow, "Make that damn bed again." That only happened once. I got the idea. Mom, you'll never have to make my bed again. I'm a pro."

That's it then, folks. Snipe hunting, deer gutting, and eggshell jokes, all in a day's work… Who knows what next month will bring?

Your loving son, Matt
July 20, 1966

Chapter 17

THE MCCANN FIRE

LATE JULY 1966 – GASQUET, CALIFORNIA

Matt Samuels finally got his wish. On a quiet July day late in the month a fire broke out on the McCann Ranch near the town of Gasquet, approximately 18-miles northeast of Crescent City. Spotted by a sharp-eyed local lumberjack, the CDF was contacted, which in turn led to Matt's station being dispatched to the fire. In less than a minute the crew was on their way.

The Crescent City CDF rig was the first one to the fire, which was burning out of control through a waist high corn field and heading directly toward a wooded area with heavy underbrush approximately 300 yards away. The cornfield torched and, whipped by a strong unsettling wind, sent sparks flying in every direction.

Pushed by Doug, the pumper truck raced along the side of the cornfield, throwing a torrent of water at the fire. The crew hurried along looking for hot spots and trying to keep sparks from igniting an adjacent dry field of wheat.

Frank could see immediately that additional crews were needed. He quickly radioed for help.

For his part, Matt had placed the McCulloch in a waterhole for cattle and was pumping out a steady stream of greenish liquid through the unrolled cotton hose into the pumper truck, which now idled near the fire. With its more forceful pump, the truck could send a stream of water further than the McCulloch alone. Even with that, little was gained on controlling this blaze.

Taking a calculated chance, Frank led his crew toward the flash point of the fire and chiseled in a pathetically thin fire line. Then, even though the wind was not as favorable as he would have like, Frank ignited a backfire. Immediately, the new fire fled toward the larger one, burning fuel as it went along. The two fires met in clash of cinders, sparks, and smoke. For a moment, there was a whirlwind of fire, and then almost magically, the singular fire seemed to extinguish itself.

The crew had gained the upper hand for a moment. "Watch out for spot fires," Frank yelled. "Keep a close eye on those woods." He need not have yelled. He had trained his crew well and his guys lived up to his hopes. They were on top of this thing.

Help finally arrived in the form of a small D-3 tractor owned by the ranch. Though its blade was only three feet across, the tractor was nimble and quickly huffed and puffed a larger fire line between the cornfield and the woods. The cat-skinner worked his machine like a fine watch. In a few minutes, he had a much wider line around the entire fire. Watching all this, Matt was mightily impressed by this little *John Deer*.

Stopping the fire and controlling it the first step in the firefighter's manual. The next step was a combination of watching for spot fires and mopping up, a dirty, time consuming job.

Released from his McCulloch, Matt was given the lead of the hose, the nozzle at the request of Frank. He was really surprised by the powerful pressure forcing the water forward. It took all his strength to hang onto the hose nozzle, which, like a bucking bronco, had a life of its own and wanted to be free of any restraints.

Mopping up meant checking out every hot spot, dousing it with water, or tossing dirt on it if not water was available. Everything was hot --- the ground, the air, the brass nozzle., the brass buttons on our Levi pants. Water poured into a hot spot ignited a stream of steaming hot air and seemingly, all the bugs in the area. Smoke and soot combined in a smelly way to almost blind Matt with tears. In no time, Matt was covered with ash and enjoyed a blackened face. He also had added a bit of a BBQ smell to himself.

Mopping up was a necessary but nasty job.

An hour into the mopping up, a second rig arrived from Smith River. After they checked us out, the crew reluctantly joined in the fun. Three hours later, Frank passed the word. "Let's eat."

MOPPING UP

A CDF jeep had brought extra large pizzas and cold drinks for the two crews, plus three apple pies, and assorted paper plates, plastic utensils, and lots of napkins. While not quite home cooking, Matt found the food delightful. Beggars couldn't afford to be choosy.

Though the fire was mainly out and pretty well mopped up, one crew had to spend the night just in case there was a flare up. Crescent City won the honors. In that way, Matt got his first nighttime duty. He found it completely boring just walking along his portion of the line and keeping a lookout for flareups.

Around midnight, Doug came by with a compliment.

"Nice work today, Matt with the McCulloch."
"Thanks."
"You did a good job with the mop up. You weren't afraid to get dirty."
"It's the little kid in me who enjoys playing in a mess."
"Whatever. Just wanted to know you're OK in my book."

The next morning a fresh crew arrived from Klamath. The boys from Crescent City went home full of themselves and the work they had done. Of course, Frank put everything into perspective when he said, "Guys, you did a dandy job. We knocked hell out of this 3-acre fire. Now just imagine this fire a hundred times larger. That would surely be one hell of a fire."

That night Matt wrote another long letter home detailing his first real experience with fire. As he sealed the envelope and stuck a stamp on it, he thought about Frank's observation. What would a fire of such a magnitude be like when fighting it? He couldn't even begin to imagine such a conflagration.. God, he thought, it must be like seeing the whole world on fire.

FIGHTING A WILDFIRE

Chapter 18

THINGS ARE HEATING UP

AUGUST 1966 – DEL NORTE COUNTY

As the last days of July departed, the temperatures leaped as predicted by the weather forecasters. Triple digit numbers were in effect. At the same time, the humidity fell through the floor, reaching a point where it was almost off the scale. The winds were picking up to, erratic and gusting air currents swooping across the mountains, screeching through tight canyons, and sweeping past low lying valleys and pastures. The land was dry. The trees were full of very flammable sap and rosin. Underbrush, which had avoided fire for many years, had grown mature and was densely populated.

The county was tinder dry.

The fire warning was extreme danger. Campers were asked to avoid campfires. Tourists were warned to use their ashtrays. Lumberjacks exercised extra caution with their equipment. The sawmills worked more carefully to avoid any chance of fire. The police were on high notice to watch out for arsonists. Parents were enjoined to monitor their kids, who just might play with matches.

The whole county was tense.

Volunteer fire departments, always serious in their self-imposed responsibilities, were even more earnest in their preparation for the "big one." Small town fire departments checked and rechecked their emergency plans, as did the CDF and the "feds."

At every airfield in the proximity of the national and state forests in Del Norte County plans were drawn up to serve CDF aircraft. This meant that borate bombers and water tankers would have a place to land, either on purpose or because of an emergency. To this end, water tanks, lakes, streambeds, and rivers were again identified and pinpointed, since a source of water was key to refilling the tankers.

Lookouts walked their isolated towers with a sense of foreboding. Theirs was an important but lonely vigil. On their maps, they knew where control-fires were, former fires, sawmills, community dumps, and just about anything that burned or smoked. If something popped, they would know it first. Perhaps it would be a lightning strike, or possibly a car accident. Then there would be the column of smoke ascending into the sky. Supporting the lookouts were the air patrols that constantly made low-level flights over the endangered forests. From sunrise to sunset, these little planes sought out what they didn't want to see. In some respects, they were like a radar officer pinging the depth and desiring no returning "bong" indicating the adversary.

Every half an hour, public service announcements were made to remind people of the fire danger on both television and radio. Already an icon in fire prevention, *Smokey the Bear* was a continuing voice and a familiar figure urging people to be careful, to protect their wilderness and to act in a responsible manner.

Throughout the CDF, support plans were designed to bring in additional crews if necessary. Stations as far away as Napa, Sonoma, and

Lake counties were put on high alert. "Be ready to drive northward if this things blows." The same effort was made with the Oregon State Division of Forestry (ODF). Crews just north of the border would be prepared, and, if necessary, thrown into the action. Uncommon, but necessary cooperation led the two states to create a unified command in the event of a "blow out."

At Matt's station the crew was relentlessly trained. Though boring, repetition refines skills and prepares a person for the unexpected. Frank and Doug seemed to be everywhere as they pushed, preached, and prodded. This crew would be ready for anything, they hoped. This effort led them one day to be even more serious than usual.

"Fire is all around you," Frank said with heightened emotion. "Your planned avenues of escape are cut off," he continued. "What do you do?"

"Cry," said one of the guys as a nervous joke.

"Call the fire department," Mike Henderson said with a big grin that gave away his anxiety.

"Run for the hills," Johnny Youngblood counseled. "Get away from the bluecoats," he muttered half jokingly.

"What'd you think Larry?" Doug asked. "You've been around a lot. What should we do?"

"Saying your prayers and getting straight with the big guy above might be in order."

"Good idea," Doug responded. "Might be a good to start now rather than wait to the last minute."

"How about you, Samuels?" Frank said with no mirth in his voice. "What would a city kid do?"

What would he do? Matt thought to himself. Tough question. As he probed for an answer, he reflected on the way Doug addressed him in comparison to Frank. Doug called him Matt. Frank referred to him as Samuels. What the hell, he thought, I know who I am.

"We're waiting, Samuels."

"There's always something you can do to resolve the problem," Matt said straightforwardly.

"So what would you do?" Frank pushed with a questioning glare. "And try to use little words for those of us who haven't been to college."

"Damn," Matt said, as he stared back at his boss with his best "you can't intimidate me look." But what would he say?

"I read some histories of wild fires in the Southwest, where fire crews were trapped. Most of the crews were rescued at the last second. But one crew out of Santa Fe was trapped in the White Mountains. Every avenue of escape was closed off by fire. They had run out of time."

"What happened," Jim Molina asked in his usual lazy draw, but this time with a sense of urgency in his voice. "Did they make it?"

"They made it."

"How?" Johnny Youngblood questioned.

And so Matt told them.

Chapter 19

LAST LETTER

MID-AUGUST 1966 – CRESCENT CITY

Dear Family,

Things are getting a little hairy here. The fire danger is off the wall. I figured I better write to you before something happens and I'm out of circulation fighting the monster fire everyone expects. But first… Mom, I'm OK. I've actually put on five pounds of muscle, not that other stuff. Lately, my asthma doesn't seem to bother me as much. That's tough to figure since I'm supposed to stay away from dust and pollen. Heck, that's all we have on a fire. Dad, thanks for agreeing to our financial plan. With your help, I might make a profit this summer. Just a little joke everybody. And, Rachel, I did meet a nice woodsy girl. Nothing serious… Just a friend to catch a drive-in movie with…

A few stories I hope you'll enjoy …

I did an Indian dance during our last fire. While mopping up, my boots became so hot I started jumping around and yelling, "Hose me down." The guy on the hose nozzle did just that. My friend, Jim, hit me with a stream of water that almost knocked me over. My boots cooled, but were they water logged. The guys referred to my antics as the Indian dance. You can see why.

During one fire when our crew had night duty, I learned how to sleep standing up. We had been on the line for two days with little sleep. I just couldn't keep my eyes open. But like a sentry, falling asleep on the line is the worst thing you can do. Other guys could be in jeopardy. The oldest guy in our crew, Larry, devised a plan to give all of us a little shut eye, and still watch the line for hot spots without Doug and Frank knowing what we were doing. This is how it works. You stick a shovel deep into the ground, up to the hilt if possible. You stand up next to your shovel and wrap your Levi jacket around it before you button up. By doing this and leaning against the shovel, you grab some shuteye and still appear to be working. I thought we'd gotten away with something until the next day when Frank asked me if Larry had taught us the "stay up and sleep trick, the oldest one in the book?"

I met some new friends. Unfortunately, they can't visit our home, at least not for a long time. We were on a lightning strike working in a rough ravine with honor inmates from San Quinton Prison. We were told we couldn't fraternize with the convicts, most of whom were Negroes. Of course, that was impossible when you're working in close quarters and need to assist each other. I learned a couple of things about people in jail. First, no one is guilty. Everyone was framed or the prosecution made a mistake. Second, every inmate wants you to make a phone call for him, or mail a letter. Naturally, we couldn't do either. You should know the inmates make great coffee. When we came out of the ravine around 3:00 a.m. one night (or day), we were wet, tired, and freezing. The inmates saved us. They took an empty 50-gallon gasoline barrel, washed it somewhat, filled it with water and heated the hell out of it before dropping in a pound of coffee, which they stirred with an ax handle. They gave my unsteady hands a paper cup full of what might be called the blackest, hottest coffee I've ever had. The coffee went down like heated syrup or a satellite splashing into the ocean. But to my cold-stiff body, it was the best coffee I've ever had.

You'll be happy about this last story. I call it "the fight which never took place." Snappy title, don't you think? Anyway, as you said, dad, there's always one tough guy who wants to fight. In my case, it was Mike Henderson, who saw himself as a John Wayne-type hero. He picked on me endlessly. He wasn't fond of guys from the city, Jews, or college riff-raff. I tried to avoid him as much as possible, but that became increasing more difficult. Things were coming to a head. Everyone knew a fight was brewing. And everyone was looking forward to it except for me. Then I got real lucky. Unknown to me at first, Doug pulled Mike into his office and pointed out I had been in jail for assault and battery. He played it up big time. I had been incarcerated for two weeks while the police decided what to do with me. They couldn't do anything until they found out if the guy I had hit would live. He did.. Doug told Jim he could fight me if he wanted to but he should think through my recent police history. He thought it through and decided it might be best to avoid a fight. I guess he didn't want to get hurt before he joined the Army at the end of the summer. So that's the story of the fight that never happened.

Doug really pulled one off with that ploy. I sure owe him one.

Well, that's it. Until I write again, stay well and remember how much I love all of you.

Your son, Matt
August 13, 1966

Part IV

DESTINY

JAP BALLOONS HIT MICH., NO DAMAGE

TANK LESSON FOR AN AIR GENERAL

DETROIT TIMES

RED LINE

V-E Cost U. S. 89,477 Dead

Windsor to Visit Britain

Japan Awaits Allied Landing

British Wait To See What

Jap Balloons Hit Michigan

Chapter 20

ARRIVAL

EARLY JANUARY 1945 – WEST COAST OF AMERICA

The balloon had arrived.

The jet stream had worked its magic. For three days, it had carried the paper balloon across the wide Pacific at elevations between 31,000 to 35,000 feet. The venting system had worked perfectly, as had the sand bags. Now, weary from its long journey, the balloon was beginning to descend ever so slowly.

Below the balloon was the rough coastline of Oregon and California. The waters of the Pacific, prodded by the Japanese current, cascaded toward the rocky shore in a splash of white foam and a fountain of spray as the tide rolled in one great wave after another littering the shoreline with driftwood. Around the mad antics of the waves were sea shells of every improbable description, and an occasional reminder of those who pleasured by the sea --- a beer bottle, the dead embers of a beach campfire, or an old pair of tennis shoes, now soaked and unlaced, its owner having disowned the canvas and rubber.

But where would the balloon make landfall?

Carried along by winds at a lower elevation, the balloon crossed the Oregon border near Brookings, a small town on Highway 101 about 25-miles from Crescent City. Floating eastward, the balloon curved southward and passed over the Smith River basin, which served both states. It dipped south by southeast. Below was Del Norte County in California, an area the Spanish had called "la tierra del norte," the "land of the north," and home to giant Redwood trees, many reaching over 350 feet. For a moment it seemed that the balloon would land here, but, shoved by fickle winds, it cruised in a northerly direction and flew over the Oregon border once more. The land below was Curry County, named for George Law Curry, the first governor of the Oregon Territory. The county shared a common border with Del Norte. It was a fertile agricultural area, where most of America's Easter lilies were grown, where cattle and sheep grazed, and lumberjacks cried, "timber."

Still the balloon didn't touch down.

The balloon, pushed by a startled tailwind, hurried eastward toward the Marble Mountains in adjacent Siskiyou County, a range of forested peaks, v-shaped ravines, and tortuous roads that ran through the unruly, but certainly beautiful topography. The area was home to the Marble Mountain Wilderness, some 250,000 acres set aside by the "feds" as a national forest to be protected from overly zealous lumber companies and those who would exhaust the land through irresponsible mining.

Each year the many lakes and streams in the national forest were stocked with steelhead trout and salmon to lure fisherman to this enchanted but rugged land. The lakes had been carved by past glacial activity as the land rose from violent upheavals spurred by volcanic eruptions eons ago.

The Marble Mountains were composed of prehistoric marine invertebrates, which once had inhabited the warm, shallow sea that gave birth to the whole area. In a climate nearly perfect for great trees to take root, they had --- the conifers, the Western juniper, the weeping spruce, the Shasta red fir, the Western white pine, and the tall ponderosa. All of them stretched skyward as the balloon floated overhead at about 3,000 feet.

Whipping through these forests, a strong breeze ruffled the trees and spoke to the balloon in whispers of falling leaves and tired limbs, all of which fell to the soft duff covering the ground.

It was as if each tree wanted the honor of snagging the balloon. Yet, the balloon flew on denying all suitors.

Descending quickly now, the balloon drifted over the small community of Happy Camp in Siskiyou County. The tiny town straddled the Klamath River near SR 96. Beyond its great fishing, the town's claim to fame rested on its past. Long ago, the area had been home to two Native American tribes, the Karuks, "the upper river people," and the Yurocks, "the downriver people." Their ancestors still roamed the land as hunting and fishing guides, and as sheepherders and cattle drivers. This was in addition to their roadside stalls, where fine, homemade jewelry was sold to tourists.

A cloudy sky framed the descending balloon against an intensely blue sky, even as the breeze calmed itself as if it were catching its breath. Flying just above the tallest trees, the balloon, like a cloud falling from the heavens, seemed to be choosing the landing site destiny had decreed for it. A tall and stately ponderosa lay just ahead of the balloon, its top branches hovering high above other trees. The great tree reached out and snagged the balloon in a tangle of lines and limbs.

The balloon finally landed.

As it hung from the ponderosa, the control box swayed back and forth before gravity took hold and inertia brought it to a stop. It just hung there and waited for the expected fuse detonation, which would release the bombs and incendiaries that would fall heavily to the ground, where an explosion would take place upon impact. The balloon waited. Inexplicably, the fuses didn't ignite. The lethal weapons were not released. No explosion occurred. The balloon just hung there swaying ever so little, a silent sentinel of a dying empire.

No coast guard observer tracked the balloon. No airline pilot observed it. No forest lookout station saw it. Ghost-like, it had found its way to America unseen by human eyes.

Once it landed, a hawk screeched by and flew on uninterested in the funny looking creature dangling in the Ponderosa. Squirrels gave it a cursory look and scurried on with their business of collecting nuts and staying out of trouble. Below a large brown bear stared up at the visitor, grunted and moved on unimpressed by the newcomer.

Later that day, the weather changed dramatically, growing colder with ominous clouds packing the sky. Two days later, the temperature dropped below freezing, and it snowed. A mantle of white fluff fell to the ground, covering the balloon in a lace-work of white, flaky crystals. A few miles away, the town of Happy Camp was coated by the same snowfall.

The balloon, restrained by the great tree, continued to hang. To all appearances it looked like a giant Christmas ornament.

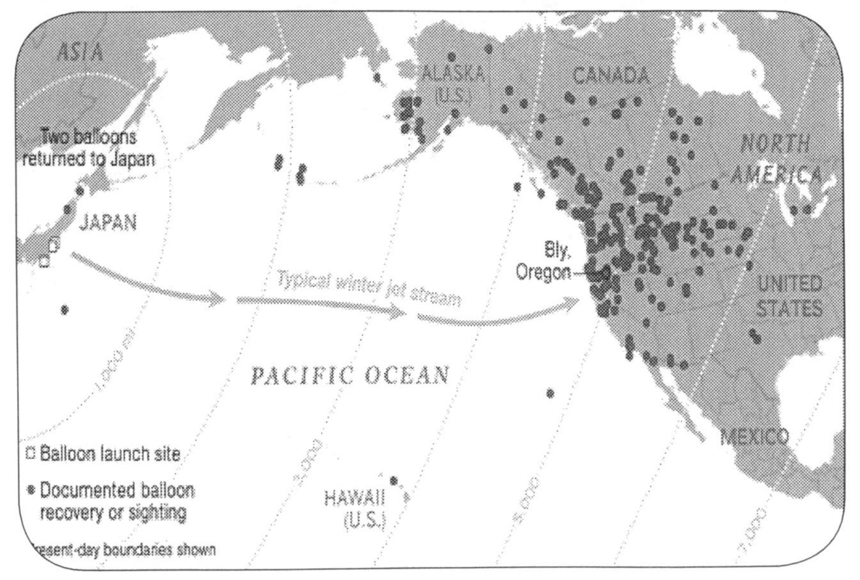

THE EASTERLY JET STREAM

Chapter 21

THE GREAT FIRE OF 1910

"Okay, you knuckleheads, listen up."

Frank was addressing the entire crew in his usual charming and benevolent manner.

""We've got a guest today, Professor Sherman. He's from our local college, Humboldt State College over in Arcata. He's here with two things in mind. I'll let him get into that. Professor…"

"Hi, guys. Let me get right to the point. I'm visiting the CDF stations hoping to recruit some of you to attend our college. Humboldt has a fine Forestry Department that you might consider if you want to stay in this firefighting business or some related field. The college needs to increase its enrollment and students need a local school. A good win-win situation, I think."

Professor Sherman was in his 50's, average height with a beguiling smile, and a few extra pounds here and there.

"Okay, the recruitment pitch is over. As you head into the worst of the fire season, Frank thought you might like to hear about the Great Fire of 1910 which burned three million acres, burning in Montana, Washington, Idaho, and British Columbia in the summer of 1910. I agree. There are lessons to be learned from that fire.

"It's sometimes referred to as the Big Blowup, the Big Burn, or the Devil's Broom Fire. This fire destroyed numerous small towns, while ruining an estimated billion dollars' worth of timber. It's considered the largest fire in American history, at least to now. The burn area was nearly he size of the state of Connecticut. I should point out that 87 people, mostly firefighters were killed fighting the inferno."

Firefighters are like Marines assaulting a beach. Every guy hopes to make it. He's got to believe that. The same is true when you battle an out-of-control fire. You just know you're going to survive. But, of course, that's not always the case. Certain jobs run a risk. The Professor's last comment quietly unwrapped that shadow.

"A lot of things contributed to the fire in 1910, very much like today, at least potentially. The wildfire season started early. The spring and summer were extremely dry. The weather was extremely hot. The humidity was correspondingly low. The forests were teeming with dry fuel due to the heavy rainfall during the previous winter. In short, the West was a tinderbox waiting to explode. It did. There were thousands of fires burning in mid-August. Any idea what happened?"

The guys were quiet, all but one who timidly offered a possible explanation.

"The fires united."

"Very good. What's your name?"

"Matt."

"Well, Matt, did you reach that conclusion?"

"Something had to occur which united the fires, otherwise the conflagration wouldn't happen?"

"Assuming you're right, what might have happened?"

"Fires are pushed by winds. Perhaps a monster storm with unbelievable winds drove the fires together."

"Very good and very correct. Hurricane-force winds whipped the hundred of small fires into one so large it was beyond the ability of firefighters to control. Eventually, thousands of untrained men would fight this fire, including 4,000 Army troops. And here's a bit of trivia for you. The troops included seven companies form the US Army's 25 Infantry Regiment. We know this group today as the Buffalo Soldiers. As a group, the outnumbered the entire black population of Idaho."

"A fire that large must have been seen for miles."

"Correct, Matt. Seen and smelled. People in Watertown, New York saw the smoke cloud. The smelled it too. The same was true in Denver, Colorado and in California. Ships some 50-miles out into the Pacific Ocean could not navigate by the stars because of the smoke."

"Sir, there is, I think another reason for your presence."

"Matt, you are an inquisitive young man. Frank wanted you to be aware of the extreme dangers you'll face this month. He wanted you to know about the 'Lost Crew' and the 'Tunnel.' He wants you to learn some lessons in survival."

This unexpected admission elicited the fullest attention from Matt's buddies. They seemed to understand that something was on the line, like perhaps their lives.

The Lost Crew

"An entire 28-mn crew was overcome by flames and perished outside of Avery, Idaho in 1910. Exactly what happened is not completely known. The great fire overtook the crew. They were warned to leave the fire line. Apparently, they believed that no real danger existed. Perhaps they thought it was safer to stay where they were. A forester, Edward Stahl, later wrote about the fire at Storm Creek.

The flames were shooting hundreds of feet into the air. They were fanned by a tornado-type wind so violent that the flames flattened out ahead, swooping to earth in great daring curves, truly a veritable red demon from hell.

"One past-fire commentary said:

You can't outrun wind and fire that are traveling 70 miles an hour. You can't hide when you are entirely surrounded by red-hot color. You can't see when it's pitch black in the afternoon. Supervisors' and rangers' official reports, old-timers' remembrances, and newspaper stories verify that on District One there were men who went stark raving crazy, men who flung themselves into the onrushing flames, men who shot themselves. It was the Big Blowup!

THE GREAT FIRE OF 1910

The Tunnel

"You already know the name Ed Pulaski. In the annals of the US Forestry he occupies an honored place. I'm not just talking about the Pulaski tool. Of more importance was what he did to save 44 men under his command.

"His crew was fighting the fire near the town of Wallace, Idaho. They were about to be overrun by the advancing fire that had already destroyed the town. Pulaski led his men to an old abandoned mine. With his men, they fought off the flames at the mouth of the shaft until most of them passed out. As the story goes, around midnight some of the men argued for leaving the mine. Pulaski, knowing that the men would not survive if they left, drew his pistol. He threatened to shoot the first person that tried to leave. In the end, only five men died. Pulaski was later called a hero for protecting his men. The mine tunnel was eventually named the Pulaski Tunnel. It is listed on the National Register of Historic Places."

Professor Sherman stopped to catch his breath and to drink some water. He did, however, ask, "Are there any questions?" Once more Matt stepped into the breach.

"There are lessons here for us, Professor?"

"Why do you say that, Matt?"

"No other explanation makes sense. You want us to be prepared for any eventuality."

"And how am I doing that?"

Matt paused before answering, then quietly said, "By telling us what to do."

"And that is?"

"First, follow orders, first and foremost. Don't charge off on your own. Second, always have an escape route in case its necessary to leave in a hurry. Third, have a final option if things get too dicey."

"Frank, you have a budding full-time CDF employee, and Humboldt may get a new student."

THE FAMOUS CAVE

Chapter 22

DETONATION

EARLY AUGUST 1966 – SISKIYOU COUNTY

Thick thunder clouds were lumbering across the sky, darkened patches of juiced up wispy lines of moisture concentrated into a solid mass of stored up energy. Booming cannon-like sounds accompanied their march across Del Norte County as they inexorably moved toward the Marble Mountains. For the folks watching this parade, it was like watching bumper-cars in the sky as the clouds seem to bump and bang into each other.

And then it began to pour great rivers of water that drenched those below. It seemed like Lake Tahoe had flipped over and drained itself on the land. It rained for two solid days causing every river in the area to reach flood stage. Many low-lying cabins were flooded out, even as natives of the area and tourists alike fled to higher ground. Rumor had it that certain religious groups were very much considering building an ark. Lookouts throughout the national forest, and others observing for the CDF could see nothing through their field glasses. They needed a giant window washer to clear the bucketful of water raining down on their purview.

Lightning accompanied armada of clouds across the sky. Bolts of freed energy lit up the night sky in jagged shafts of light, as if a crazed javelin thrower had gone mad and sought to impale his spear into the very earth. Strangely, no lightning strike was recorded. It was as if the earth had an invisible shield to ward off the bolts.

Together with the thunder and rain, it seemed like the gods were dancing to some airy tune, which, at the moment, would be played out above the land. On the second day, the storm reached a crescendo. The sky was literally tearing itself apart.

Then everything stopped --- the lightning, the thunder, and the rain. All ceased. The silence that followed was deafening. People emerged from their homes to witness a night sky quickly clearing itself of the stormy clouds. Everywhere there were puddles of water, if not more. The land was saturated. A full moon peered out of the night sky. No one could remember such a bright moon or weather like this.

It was around 8:30 p.m. that it happened. A clap of thunder boomed in an empty sky save for the stars that twinkled and blinked in the firament that marked the hand of creation. For a moment the world was still. Then a lightning shaft burst forth from the heavens and careened downward toward the Siskiyou National Forest. The lightning lit up the night and unerringly found its mark. It rocketed into the tallest tree it was drawn to, a great ponderosa. It smacked into the tree just above where a balloon had quietly hung for twenty-one years.

The bolt devastated the great tree. It was split right down the middle. Its branches and limbs shuddered under the impact and then leaped from their host to only fall quickly to the ground. Some were on fire as they did so. The lightning peeled the bark right off the Ponderosa and lit a fire within the tree. It was now a potentially dangerous snag.

Electricity flowed through the tree to the balloon's control box like a hand-operated plunger to ignite TNT. Currents of electricity made contact. A connection was made. The dormant box activated causing the fuse to finally burn. A moment later a small charge detonated to free the two previously inert bombs and two incendiaries. It was as the old war machinery had finally gone "click." The bombs fell to the ground. Most of the tiny arsenal landed in soft, water soaked moss and peat, the duff of the forest floor. But one bomb hit a large rock near the tree. It was enough. For a long moment, there was no sound. The forest seemed to be holding its breath.

A mini-second later the bomb exploded and ignited the other weapons. Together they made a large explosion. To those in Happy Camp, it sounded like two freight trains colliding. Immediately following, there was a flash of fiery light, which dissipated quickly. A sense of unease pervaded the town. What had happened? Did a plane crash? Was it a freak lightning show? Had the Martians finally landed, H.G. Wells notwithstanding?

Of course, the old timers in Happy Camp had all the answers. There was nothing to worry about. The storm had passed. The ground would dry. Life would go on.

"Joe, nothing to worry about. The ground is so wet, you'd need a volcano to start a fire."

"I guess you're right, Ben."

"Sure I am. You've never seen lightning start a fire in a lake."

"Only if it hits the boat."

"You've got me there, Joe."

"Hell, let's have a beer."

"Why not?"

Ben, it seemed, was right. There was no smoke to be seen. The lightning strike was a dud.

Twenty miles away, the lookout at Alder Point noted where the lightning hit. A second lookout on Boulder Peak, rising well over 8,000 feet in the Marble Mountains, confirmed the sighting. A third lookout at Hungry Point in Oregon also filed a report. The three sightings were triangulated.

The bolt had hit five miles north of Happy Camp.

Throughout three counties, del Norte, Siskiyou, and Curry, men and machines prepared to battle a yet unseen fire. Days off were cancelled. All crews were on standby. Patrol planes were fueled and staffed. Water tankers brimmed with their precious cargo. Borate bombers lined the runway at two military bases in the Bay Area. The big "cats: were loaded onto their transports. The cat-skinners checked and rechecked their equipment. The media was alerted. Reporters were awakened.Old maps of the area were pulled out. Where the hell was Happy Camp?

An army was preparing to do battle.

The word had come to the Crescent City CDF crew. Head eastward just in case. Other crews were told to move northward. The Klamath crew came to Crescent City. The crew from Weott moved into the Klamath station. In turn, the Garberville crew replaced them. And so on it went. The chess pieces were on the move.

Frank had anticipated the move. An hour earlier he had turned into a whirling dervish.

"Get your sleeping bags on the rig. Take extra clothes. Biscuits, we'll need extra sandwiches. Don't forget the canteens. Take extra ones. Write any last postcards. Use the office phone, if you want to. But hurry."

Matt remembered "but hurry" sounding more like, "move your ass!" Within a few minutes of the word to head eastward, they were on the road. A moment before for reasons he didn't understand, Matt stuck his tongue out and tasted the wind. He pulled it back almost immediately. It felt singed though there was no fire. He felt like he had a mouth full of ash. He looked around. What the heck was going on?

In the main CDF base in Fortuna, one question haunted the strategists who would conduct this war from their planning room. "Did they have a "sleeper fire" on their lands?

The wet, spongy ground absorbed much of the blast much like a mattress might with a string of large firecrackers exploding on it. It did, however, leave a crater of considerable size in which a tiny fire smoldered in the duff thrown up by the blast. As for the incendiaries, they lit and burned furiously in the damp and heavy shrubbery. The incendiaries failed to ignite more than a few twigs.

The embryonic fire was on life support. At this exact moment, it was barely able to live. One pail of water would have put it out completely.

It was indeed a sleeper fire," one that needed only a small nudge to evolve into a conflagration. It appeared dead. But it wasn't. The spark of life still lived in the little flame barely able to heat itself.

For two days the fire fought to live in the quickly drying land. Just when it was about to go out, a gentle breeze would spring it back to life. Just when there was no fuel left to burn, a squirrel would go by and kick leaves into the gasping flame. As such, the fire was barely surviving this precarious life, but three things, each unexpected and unseasonable, happened in rapid succession to offer salvation.

First, like a NASA rocket seeking the heavens, the temperature shot up to over 110 degrees in the shade. Second, the humidity dove in the opposite directions, seeking an improbable zero on the scale measuring moisture in the air. Third, the wind stampeded. Gusts roared and blew down through the many mountain ravines and over the high passes of the Marble Mountains. The wind lapped the glacial lakes in the area and forged ahead bending brush and grass before it as it moved unimpeded. Like a giant hair dryer, it heated up the land, purging it of moisture, leaving it dry as a bone.

Eventually, the heated winds found the balloon fire.

The wind refreshed the fire. It blew moss into the fire and small pieces of kindling. That was enough. Embers flared and the wind caught them and hurled them out of the creator in every direction. Soon there were little fires in a small concentrated area. Each one reached out for more grass, pine cones, twigs, and then larger branches and the heavy foliage. The fire sprouted yellow flames and made crackling sounds, even as white smoke tunneled upward. The little fires expanded and found each other in a family reunion of sorts.

In a Darwinian world of survival, the fire had. Wind, heat, and very low humidity were its allies. But to live, the fire would have to spread to constantly satisfy its need for fuel to burn. It was a creature of expansion, not constriction.

The fire was now one acre, but it had reached critical mass. It was close to being self-sustaining. It was beginning to generate its own heat. To a lesser degree, it was creating its own air draft. It was a dangerous, luminous foe that moved without passion or morality. It simply existed. It did what was expected of it. It burned all before it.

It was no longer a timid creature of nature.

Within an hour, the fire would close on ten acres. It was in the heavy brush now and stalking small trees. It was eating into the sap and rosin in the trees, the napalm of nature, which only increased fires intensity. Igniting the sap caused the little trees to literally explode. The fire now burned in every direction. It had escaped to become an uninhibited creature of its own nature.

It had become a wildfire.

The three lookouts saw the smoke at almost the same time. Their reports were flashed to the waiting army. The word went out. War was declared.

Eventually, the Happy Camp fire would burn for three weeks and immolate over 250,000 acres of prize timber and grazing land.

It would threaten five towns in two states, most notably Happy Camp. To the west, Crescent City prepared for the worst. To the north, Brookings saw the red skies and thick clouds and wondered if the inferno could be stopped. Two small Oregon towns, O'Brien and Takima were evacuated.

Over 3,000 firefighters took on the monster. Crews came from as far south as San Diego, as far east as Arizona and New Mexico, as far north a the Puget Sound area. Every available man was thrown into the battle. At one time or another, there were three-dozen "D-8 and D-9 cats" on the line. Their eight to ten foot blades carved out miles of fire-line.

The fire was blitzed from the air, too. Though limited to daylight attacks, the water tankers were everywhere attempting to knock down flare-ups. The borate bombers poured tons of suppression chemicals on the trees and thick brush, trying desperately to land the reddish stuff just in front of the fire in an attempt to deny the inferno the fuel it needed.

When the firestorm occurred and the fiery flames reached the tree tops and crowned, defeat stared harshly at the weary defenders. Burning at tree top level, the fire raced ahead unchallenged. Base camps were forced to move three times. The fire had crowned.

Equipment and men were pulled back again and again. Where possible, backfires were started in front of the wall of flames. Still, the fire burned and destroyed. Structures and homes were devoured. Lumber mills and recreational cabins and resorts were threatened. Great swaths of prime lumber were turned into ash. The watershed itself was at risk.

It was impossible to tell how many animals died. Whatever the number, it was atrociously high. The smell of burned flesh gave mute testimony to the murderous power of the fire. Conservationists and their kin, the environmentalists, were appalled by the terrible toll the fire was taking on the natural habitat and wildlife.

Seemingly, nothing could stop the fire. Man did not have the capacity or the power to stop it. The fire would burn until it ran out of fuel.

And then it rained.

For two days, a soft rain fell on the fire quieting its terrible temper. As the fire cooled, firefighters threw a great Chinese wall --- a firebreak --- around their adversary. Hot spots were descended upon and spot fires were quickly put out. The mopping up operations took two weeks. Only then was the Happy Camp fire declared controlled and out.

Thousands of firefighters had earned their modest wages. Hundreds had been injured in the fierce fight. Three had died.

The Happy Camp fire was now history.

All of this hadn't happened yet when the crew from Crescent City arrived at the fire. Ahead of them were experiences they could not have imagined in a thousand years. The fire would test them as nothing else had ever done. In the coming days, they would learn a lot about fire, and even more about themselves.

The "Boys of Crescent City" were about to become men.

IGNITED BY A BALLOON BOMB

Chapter 23

ON THE LINE

MID-AUGUST 1966 – MARBLE MOUNTAINS

The Crescent City crew was the first station to reach the fire. According to CDF records, the fire was about fifteen acres at that time. Though relatively small, it was raging in an area that had had no major fire for over 40-years. Consequently, the underbrush was extremely thick and with the prevailing strong gusty wind, there would be no dearth of fuel for the fire.

Frank quickly sized things up as he radioed in to Fortuna. "The sleeper fire has become a wild fire."

Against his better thinking, Frank took a chance. The pumper truck raced along an old logger's road to reach the head of the fire. Still on the flank of the fire, the guys tried to put in a firebreak in an attempt to slow the fire. Being this close to the "front" was always a dangerous thing to do. It proved to be an effort in futility. The undergrowth --- mainly Manzanita --- was just too thick and primed to explode as embers and sparks flew at and over the absurdly small two-foot wide firebreak the crew feverishly cleared. The fire sniffed the "break" and leaped over it with distain.

The crew was forced to retreat.

And that's the way it was for the next two weeks. The crew – now part of a 3,000-man force fighting the Happy Creek Fire --- was constantly on the move, going from one hot spot to another, or attacking spot fires around the clock at the beckoning of hurried and frantic CDF calls. During those two weeks, the fire literally blew up. It was an inferno, Dante's vision realized in the Klamath River Basin.

A later review of action seen by the crew indicated the station was on fourteen hot spots within burned out areas and eleven spot fires caused by the fire jumping firebreaks. The records, of course, didn't mention the lack of sleep, the continuous physical exertion, and the numerous injuries from bruises, cuts, and sprained ankles in addition to mainly first-degree burns. Nor did the records total the cotton hose damaged or ruined beyond repair, or the damage done to the pumper by falling limbs and sharp rocks that shredded the rig's tires.

All this occurred along with other slights. Boots were the first to go. Constantly in use in the rugged terrain, and too water-logged for their own good, the soles gave way after two weeks. Repairs, such as they were, took place on the run. A common fix was to use "duct tape" to keep sole and boot together in a tenuous relationship. Heels were another matter. If they came off, you worked lopsided.

Clean woolen sox were a thing of the past after ten days. You merely used the same dirty, smelly socks again and again on a rotating basis. The tan, cotton shirts and Levi pants simply absorbed the dirt and ash that played upon them. A clean starched shirt was only a distant memory. Unwashed the Levi jacket slowly became something akin to armament worn by knights during the Middle Ages.

The crew felt isolated. Though thousands of men were on the fire, the crew only knew its tiny piece of the puzzle. The world was condensed into this spot fire, or that blow up. They never knew the "big picture," though they knew the picture was big.

Their world was limited to eating, sleeping, and fighting fire day after day. There was no respite.

"S's'" defined their existence. Little sleep. No showers. Too much smoke. And the word "shit" replaced other possible ways to describe life on the line.

If the fire was a horror, the camp food was great once you were pulled off the fire.

Breakfast was a treat. Two large pancakes coated with slabs of butter and thick syrup together with a mound of scrambled eggs and a load of very cooked bacon filled stomach. A can of juice and a cartons of milk were available if you didn't want to chance the black coffee.

Dinner, especially if the "feds" were paying the bill, might include a large steak, heaping portions of mashed potatoes, an ear of corn, lots of government surplus beans, bread and the usual drinks. Lunch was a mess. Brown bags were in, as were the baloney sandwich, tiny can of juice, a piece of fruit, and a very dry cookie. The baloney was stuck between two weak slices of white bread with a light smear of mayo and a hint of mustard. You had to be really hungry not to reject the offering.

It seemed like the men were always hungry.

On the days when the fire camp ran for its life because of the advancing fire, there were no hot meals. On such days, old military K-rations were in and dreadfully accepted with the greatest reluctance.

As for the fire, it bobbed and weaved when it wasn't strutting and prancing. Mohammad Ali had nothing on this fire.

The usual plan of attack had simplified itself to one strategy. Almost always, a big D-8 tractor would crunch out a line and the crew would follow the clanking, metal treads watching for flare-ups and spot fires. It wasn't too unlike the infantry following behind a tank to take on a pillbox.

If there was a difference, the enemy might surrender. The fire didn't know the meaning of the word.

A BIG CAT AT WORK

If the fire in your area couldn't be contained, exact coordinates were radioed in and, if you were fortunate, a water tanker appeared out of the clouds to make a drop. At other times a borate chemical, orange and reddish in color, was dropped on the advancing fire. The chemical suffocated the fire by preventing combustion. It acted as a fire retardant when the winds were favorable and visibility was good.

Throughout his time on the Happy Camp Fire, Matt kept a diary in order to maintain his equilibrium. After a few days, he gave up on noting the date. The days had simply merged and congealed into an amorphous mass. He simply numbered the days.

DAY 5 - Today was a rough one. We were assigned the job of clearing a meadow of seven snags, which were burning on the inside, while throwing out embers and sparks from a hollowed opening, usually toward the top of the trees. The fire had burned through these trees, but it hadn't burned them down. They were a constant danger to start spot fires. They had to come down.

DEALING WITH A HOT SPOT

If a D-8 were around, the big tractor would slam into the snag in an attempt to knock the weakened tree off its roots. There was always a splash of sparks upon impact, either with the tractor or the ground if the tree was toppled. Once down, the snag had to be pulled out of the fired over area and soaked with water or buried with as much sand as was available.

Getting the snag out of the area was dirty, tiring work. You had to set a "choker" around the snag. This was a length of heavy cable, something like a noose a condemned man might enjoy on the gallows. Once placed on the snag, the choker was connected to a longer chain that ran to the tractor's winch, which, once turned on, pulled the snag toward it.

Gloves were a necessity for this kind of work. The choker was hot. The cable connection was hot. The larger cabled connected to the winch was hot. The gloves protected you from the heat and also strands of cable wire that had eroded away from the parent cable and were extremely sharp.

If no "cat" was available, a CDF guy would come in with a portable saw and go at it. This was dangerous work. Except for his helmet, he was unprotected from falling limbs, sparks and embers. We would try to spot for him. We called the falling stuff widow-makers for obvious reasons.

DAY 8 – I became a truck driver today. Our driver, Doug, is temporarily out of commission. He suffered near second-degree burns on his hands when he tried to aid Mike Henderson, the tough guy, who was caught under a snag when he was setting a choker.

Frank asked me to drive the pumper. I was given a quick, thirty-second introduction to the nuances of double-clutching the gearshift and working the many low gears, and finally, how to run, if necessary, the winch. Once I got the hang of it, it was kind of fun. My driving time is limited to fire and logger trails, an occasional county road, or a rancher's gravel pathway. It would be great to drive on 101, flat-out with the lights blinking and the siren screaming. What a fantasy!

No one asked me for a license. I don't think anyone gives a damn about who is at the wheel.

I used the winch just once. We were caught in an almost v-shaped ravine. The rig's four-wheel drive couldn't handle the grade, either backing up or going forward. On the rise before us was a sturdy old oak, which we set a choker to in nothing flat. The winch whined and howled as I slowly wound in the cable, which in turn pulled the pumper forward. It worked; It was hot and dirty work.

DAY 11 – I became a pyromaniac last night. A cat-skinner needed someone to ride on the back of his D-8 and to throw out phosphorous grenades in order to start a large backfire. With nothing else on my social calendar, I volunteered.

I was strapped to the D-8 with a jerry-rigged seatbelt affair and off we went. For the next three hours, I lobbed grenades when given the high sign. My restraints were certainly needed. That tractor went up and down the firebreak all night at angles I thought impossible. My baseball years as a pitcher sure came in handy. After a while, I was yelling weird baseball talk as I threw the grenades --- "Strike three, Ruth. You're out!" --- "Show me what you've got, Mays" --- Try this on for size, DiMaggio." I had a no hitter going by the time we finished. I think I was in danger of becoming a pyromanic.

DAY 16 – The television people showed up today, cameras and all. Apparently, they wanted to follow one crew for a day to see how the average firefighter coped with the work. Frank admonished us to avoid using the "S-word," or we would never make the 6-O'Clock news. The television people were from KRON in San Francisco.

True to their word, they followed us all day, one that was particularly hot and dirty as we were working on a hot spot threatening to jump over the firebreak. Twice during the day, we considered backing off. The blaze was just too hot. But with cameras filming, Frank was most reluctant to leave the field. Truth be told, all of us were hamming it up for the camera, though that really wasn't necessary. The reality of the burn overwhelmed all.

For some reason, the television people choose to interview me. I explained I was from San Francisco and this was my summer job before attending CAL. When I was asked if I was afraid of the fire, I screwed up my courage and said, "Only if the fire was wild and too close, or we're trapped with no way to extricate ourselves." Extricate was a nice college word. I guess I was trying to impress the interviewer. I was also asked how I felt physically. My answer was not meant to impress anyone. "I don't I've ever been in such good physical shape, or this damn tired."

Of course, I knew I would never see the interview. Television reception was unlikely on the line. But I did wonder who might see it.

"Mom, it's time for the evening news," Rachel yelled. "Call Dad."

Rachel, Matt was told later, was home for the weekend to wash her clothes, and to enjoy her mother's great cooking and her dad's attempts at humor. The family gathered together to watch the news. It was a tradition in the household to keep up on current events. That happens when your father is a reporter and your mother is an English teacher.

The family watched the national news first, which ended with LBJ grimly noting "the need for more troops in Vietnam to meet the challenge thrown down by the Viet Cong and the North."

Next came the local and state news, which began with, "Tonight we bring you an up close look at one group of firefighters struggling to stop the wild fire in the Marble Mountains that has already consumed over 135,000 acres."

"Mom, look," Rachel exclaimed, as she almost fell out of her chair. "Isn't that Matt?"

"No, " her mother said, "that person is too old."

"Dad, what'd you think?"

Robert Samuels knew it was his son. He had seen tired, gaunt looking men before --- young men who had aged quickly. He had seen the same faces in the South Pacific. He knew the look. Boys, young men pushed too far.

"It's Matt," he said.

"Matt doesn't have a beard," his mother stated quickly. "That person hasn't shaved in days."

The interview with Matt was shown. Because of the close up shots, there was no mistaking him.

"He's changed," Rachel said. "He looks so different."

"He is different," his father said. "Work like this will do that to a man."

The camera pulled backward after the interview to show a wall of fire, seemingly everywhere. The old RCA set seemed almost unable to contain the conflagration. The fire appeared in its most terrorizing form --- a mass of malignant energy consuming all in its wake. It was a frightening spectacle.

"My, God," Rachel said. "Look at that."

"Robert, I want my son home," his mother cried out.

"What?"

"You heard me. Use your connections. But just get our boy away from that thing --- that fire."

"Mom …" Rachel muttered.

"I want my son."

"Even if I could, I wouldn't. He would never forgive us."

"How can you say that? He's in danger."

"He'll survive. He's well trained. No lives have been lost."

"He looks haggard," Rachel said.

"Please, Robert," do what you can."

Robert Samuels left the request hanging in the air. There was nothing to be done. The boy was on a fire. When it was out, he would return to his station. When the summer was over, he would return on a Greyhound bus. Until then…

To avoid further discussion, he went to the mailbox in front of the house, where he picked up the day's mail. As was his custom, he shuffled through the mail mentally thinking what needed to be thrown away, what should be kept. He stopped suddenly when he came across one piece of mail. He looked at it hard and long before folding it in half and placing it is his back pocket, almost as if he were hiding it.

As he reentered the house, he heard his daughter say, "Don't cry, mom. Matt will be fine."

"What's happening, Frank?"

"Matt, the fire is crowning."

A chill crawled up Matt's back. He had heard about a fire crowning high up in the combustible canopy of the forest, the most dangerous type of fire. It literally exploded in the sky, then to race across the landscape faster than a pumper truck could roll. It was a river of fire destroying all before it. Almost nothing can stop it.

Chapter 24

TRAPPED

LATE AUGUST 1966 – LITTLE BEAR MEADOW

By the third week of the Happy Camp Fire, it was 70% contained. The latest firebreaks were holding and hot spots were being attacked 24/7. The most recent weather reports were promising. A cooling trend would set in two days and there was an outside chance of rain. The winds were projected to decline in velocity. In a general sense, thing were looking up.

The major cause for alarm was an area about seven miles southeast of Little Bear Meadow where the fire was threatening cabins and a large resort. A strong firebreak had been put in, which extended in a half loop around the fire's front. In addition, a second line was going in close to Little Bear Meadow in case the primary firebreak failed.

And the damn fire was crowning.

THE FIRE CROWNS

In Fortuna tired CDF planners reviewed their ever-changing strategy.

"Will the Little Bear firebreak hold, Wilson?"

"As of now, Mr. Anderson, it's a 50/50 proposition," the aide said to the Director of the CDF.

"Hell, I can get better odds than that at the Klamath Casino."

"True, sir, but the casino isn't on fire."

"What about Little Bear Meadow?"

"Chancy. We have one crew there from Crescent City. We trying to get another rig up there."

"What's the hold up, Wilson?"

"Everyone is on the line somewhere. There's a three-man pumper from San Diego that's been dispatched. That's about all we can do."

"Water tankers?"

"Flying non-stop, sir."

"Keep them advised of the situation at Little Bear Meadow. If necessary, they might have to make a drop."

"The coordinates have been determined and radioed to all planes in the area. But you know the problem, don't you, sir? How do they hit a small target in gusty winds with smoke obscuring their vision?"

The Director just shrugged. He knew the problems.

"What about the borate bombers?" he asked Wilson.

"Same story."

"Christ, what a mess. Okay, no matter what, the lines south of Little Bear Meadow must be held. If fire gets into the meadow and flashes northward into the dense forested area north of it, we'll be chasing this fire all the way to Portland. That crew has got to protect the meadow. We can't let this fire flank us."

"Crowning. The word sent shivers through Matt. He knew why. The fire was now traveling above them, going from tree to tree, exploding in the canopy high above and endangering all below. He recalled reading that:

The fire burns like a temper, as if the leaping flames have a terrible anger toward the living world. It moves faster than a person can run through the deer stand a strong chance, moving swiftly as they do. The air smells and tastes life bonfire while the horizon glows orange beneath the smokey wind-dragged plume.

At Little Bear Meadow, the crew, minus Doug, had settled in awaiting orders from Frank. Doug was in a hospital in Eureka being treated for the second degree burns to his hands.

"We're in a tight fix here, guys, Frank said. There's no getting around that. There's fire coming from the south and we're its target; make no mistake about that. That's a bulls-eye you feel on your back. Only the fire lines they are putting in now stands between the fire and us. We've been told to hold here and stop any fires from taking out the meadow and then getting into the stand of trees that pretty much encircle us. We can't leave. We can't go back along the logging road that got us here. The fire will block off that avenue. The old road, really a path the rancher put in years ago, strays to the north, but it goes through the woods. We can't use that way either. We'd be trapped in there."

Frank stopped to catch breath. The word "trapped" hung in the air. For the first time, the young men, who always thought of themselves as immortal, felt little hairs of fear climbing up their backs. They hadn't counted on this when they took on this summer job.

"Okay, this is the plan," Frank said in his best boss voice with a clipped cadence. "Listen up. We're short-handed. Were going to divide into three groups. Matt, you stay with the rig and work the pumps. Johnny, you handle the hose. Try to drive along the western edge of the meadow. Hit anything that comes your way. Got it?"

"Yes," Matt said. "Right, Frank."

"10-4."

"Larry, you and Jim take the McCulloch over to that water hole. Suck up whatever you can with your baby. You man the pump Larry and Jim you handle the hose. Same deal as the rig. OK?"

"We got it," Larry said before turning to Jim. "Hey big guy, you grab the McCulloch. I'm too old for that. I'll take the hose."

"That leaves me and Mike. We'll cover that old snag there. Maybe we can bring it down. It's burning within and throwing sparks everywhere. Mike, you grab the chainsaw and I'll do the cutting. You spot for me."

A SNAG BURNING WITHIN

The plan was in place. It provided a sense of security and activity. The crew knew what they were going to do and why. They knew that, if they did it right, the fire wouldn't destroy the meadow and those in it. Still, a probing sense of unease climbed into their minds and refused to remain silent.

What they didn't know, of course, was the larger plan in operation. They couldn't know that fingers of the main fire, propelled by exceedingly high winds, was moving northwest toward Little Bear Meadow. They knew that a double line was hurriedly being put into place to block the red menace. They didn't know if it would hold. No one knew if it would hold. If the fire reached them, they didn't know if they could hold it off. And, if they couldn't hold back the fire what then? If they were in real trouble, did the CDF have a plan to help them? If they couldn't hold, should they chance the woods? Should they chance the old rancher's road?

There were too many iffy questions.

The three groups took their positions. The boys of Crescent City waited.

Above them, they saw the water tankers heading southward. Good, they thought. Flood the monster. Drown the monster. Kill the monster. In the distance, they saw a huge plane, a borate bomber, they thought, making a wide turn before commencing its drop. Again, they shouted within themselves, good. Suffocate it. Choke the life out of it. Strangle it.

WATER TANKER

An hour went by and then they heard it, a rumbling sound of an explosion and they knew what it meant. The fire had erupted, burst past the lines and tore into the sap-rich trees, which were exploding like firecrackers. A firestorm was coming their way. How long would it take before it burned its way seven miles? Not long enough, thought Matt.

"Shit," Matt said. The lines are buckling. We're in for it now, Johnny."
"My ancestors will protect us."
"But I'm not a member of your tribe."
"I make you an honorary member if you'll promise to marry my sister."
"The good looking one?"
"The other one, Matt."
"I need to think about this."

They both laughed nervously.

"Check the sky," Matt said.
"Unbelievable," Johnny muttered.

The sky was full of ash and cinders, and sparks and embers. It was as if the sky was a mattress and the feathers were pouring out, half on fire. And the wind, like some giant conveyer belt, was carrying them forward. The ash especially gave the appearance of an early snowfall. Flakes of it were falling from the sky four months before Christmas.

Fate now took charge. In the next three minutes, three unintended, impossible to predict events took place. First, a large limb fell off the snag that Frank was trying to cut down. It hit him with a sickening whack and knocked him to the ground. He lay there unconscious. Second, Larry, the old guy, finally fell prey to his forty-five years of hard work. He collapsed. The smoke and heat had gotten to him. Third, a rig from San Diego showed up with three people. They took one look at what was happening and poured on the gas, heading for the dirt road through the woods. They paid no attention to Matt, who yelled, "Not that way."

With the firestorm advancing on them and without their leaders, Doug and Frank, the guys turned to Matt. "What should we do?" they asked as a chorus. Somehow he had been elected to lead the guys.

What should they do he thought to himself? The options flirted through his mind and were just as quickly dismissed. They couldn't go back. They couldn't go forward. The rancher's road was an enticing trap.

What had he told Frank that day? He tried desperately to remember. They had agreed it was the only thing to do. He closed his eyes and stuck out his tongue, ever so slightly and tried to taste the wind. And then he knew what had to be done.

He barked his commands. "Grab Frank and take him to the waterhole. Someone help Larry. I'll bring the truck. Johnny, take the flares and light the grass behind us as we go."

"Use the flares?"
"Burn as much as you can. Take away the monster's food."
"But..."
"Do it."

The crew headed for the waterhole caring for their human cargo, Larry and Frank. There they found almost all the water gone, evaporated, or used. It didn't matter. The pond, really a waterhole, was nearly dry. Behind them came Matt. He braked and yelled, "Cover your faces with the wet mud and then these blankets. Before they did this, he turned on the rig's pump, gained pressure and hosed everyone down with the remaining water in the tank. "Get on the ground, face down, where the oxygen will be. Pair up."

Before joining his buddies, Matt sent out a radio message. "Crew needs help now --- Little Bear Meadow." He hoped the message got through past the static he heard. Thankfully, Frank had shown him how to use the radio in an emergency. Certainly, this qualified as an emergency.

He spread mud over his face and joined the crew on the ground. There was nothing more that could be done. Well, there was one thing. For the first time in his life, Matt Samuels really prayed.

Miles away in Fortuna, the Director was given the latest news from Little Bear Meadow.

"They've hunkered down, sir."
"The secondary fire line?"
"Impeding, the fire."
"Trapped? The Crescent City crew?"
"Yes, sir."
"Water tankers?"
"Making a run in three minutes."
"Borate bomber?"
"Seven minutes."
"Smoke?"
"Dense."
"Fire?"
"Close."

The crew had indeed hunkered down. Grouped next to the almost dried up water hole, they kept their handkerchiefs over their mud-splattered faces. Around them the grass had mainly burned and the fire was off in a mad dash for the woods. They were a tiny, soaked island of life in a world of fire.

With hearts pounding and coughing from the smoke-filled air, they maintained their self-control even though they were half-blinded by the same smoke. They tried not to pant or whimper. They tried to act strong, to avoid hysteria. The kept their noses close to the ground, to avoid suffocation from a lack of air. They felt the heat and wondered how hot would it get before their lungs burned. They felt hot spots on their clothes. The metal buttons on their Levi jackets and pants heated. Their metal helmets warmed seriously to the touch.

They resisted the urge to get up and run.

To Matt, it seemed like he was in a dream. Time slowed down for him. He tried to calm himself. He had been in tight places before.

There was the Division I high school playoff game at Kezar Stadium. Less than 20-seconds were left in the game. His team was on the one-yard line. Three feet, a mere 36-inches separated his team from victory. The coach called for a quarterback sneak. He placed his hands under the backside of the center and hoped he wouldn't screw up the count. "Hike." The ball was jammed into his hands. Closing his eyes, he dug his cleats into the turf and pushed forward with all his strength. Arms grabbed at him or stabbed at the ball that he held onto for dear life. He heard the grunting and cursing, and finally a whistle. Under the pile of bodies, players still scratched and kicked him to get control of the ball before the referees uncovered the pile. It seemed like ages before he heard the friendly home crowd roar. Apparently, he had covered the longest yard of his life.

They could hear it now. It was so close. A solid wall of fire was approaching them. The fire had finally reached the boundaries of Little Bear Meadows. But they could not look at it. They dared not look at it. They ground their faces into the dirt and ash, and what moisture there remained.

If help was going to come, it had to come now. He recalled another tight spot.

It was the 9th-inning. There were two outs, but the bags were loaded thanks to a walk, an error, and a solid single to leftfield. Exhausted by the game, Matt stood on the mound and wiped his perspiration off his face and out of his eyes. The best hitter for the other team was up. The count was three and two. The next pitch would tell the whole story. Did he still have any gas, Matt thought to himself, or was it over and time for someone to relieve him out of the bullpen? Logic said yes, but pride resisted. Just one more pitch, he thought. Throw the little ball sixty-feet and watch the ball crunch into the catcher's glove and the umpire signaling, "strike three." Just one more pitch… He grasped the ball tightly, reared back, and threw …

The pilot of the water tanker was taking too many chances. Unable to see Little Bear Meadow because of the dense smoke, he was flying low, too low for safety, but he had to be sure. If only the smoke would clear for a moment. And then magically it did. He was almost on top of the meadow. He pulled the release knob and hundreds of gallons fell from the sky. At the last second, he pulled up and barely missed a wooded area already burning and headed home. As he did, he prayed he had been in time.

Almost four minutes later a borate bomber flew over the area and coated the fire with a reddish chemical, a retardant to slow the fire, cool the fire, smother the fire. The pilot was unsure if he had been on target.

BORATE DROP

In Fortuna, the Director wanted answers.

"Sir, we don't know."
"Get copter teams in there."
"Already done."

The fire swept pass the pitiful huddle of firefighters from Crescent City, who had burrowed into the ground, seeking what refuge they could in the suddenly very dampened dirt that --- astonishingly --- now suddenly seemed a curious red color. They had felt the sweep of the fire as it raged around them, fiery tongues of licking flames seemingly searching them out, almost as if it knew they were there somewhere in the smoke --- clinging to life --- and hiding from its hot breath.

They had heard the fire first, as if a thousand belching, black locomotives thundered past them on invisible tracks. The fire howled and yapped, and barked as it plunged ahead like a mad dog feasting on the earth's flesh. And then came the wind and a torrent of white-hot cinders, glistening embers, and chalky ash, all of which floated over them before beginning a downward spiral that pelted them in rushing cascade of incendiary bites, each of which burned into their clothing and scorched their skin and sought their souls.

And then the fire was gone and it was eerily quiet.

Matt felt like he was waking from a dream on a distant planet, perhaps Mars. Nothing was recognizable. The landscape was covered with ash and a strange reddish stain that stung the eyes and irritated the skin. There were puddles of water all around him. Where had all the water come from? For the life of him, he couldn't remember. And this red stuff... The ground was supposed to be shades of brown and green, not red. Why was the ground red? His irritated mind sought an answer and received none. He wondered if this planet had showers. He desperately wanted to take a shower, a nice, long hot shower. That much he knew.

Other forms were stirring around him. They appeared to be earthlings, but it was difficult to be sure. They were covered in ash, he thought. Why would they be covered like that? They seem dazed. They could hardly move. They reminded him of the Pillsbury "doughboy" walking in coconut butter. Why was he thinking that? They looked so silly stumbling around, barely able to walk. He gazed more intently at them. They seemed familiar to him, yet he couldn't remember who they were? If they had names, he couldn't recall them. They seemed to be talking, but he couldn't make sense out of what they were saying. Nothing seemed to make sense. He couldn't even remember how he got to this strange place.

He wondered if this was how it felt when you go off your rocker? Or when you're dead? If this was death, he wasn't very happy about it. He didn't feel dead. He just felt dirty. But, if this were death, he would have preferred a clean room and clean clothes and to have taken a hot shower and scrubbed his skin squeaky clean before meeting his maker. That wasn't too much to ask, was it?

As to madness… As he gave thought to this possibility a strange noise collided with his ears. A motor, a powerful motor was hovering above him from the sound it was making. The noise assaulted his ears and broke the momentary stillness. He looked up and saw a glass bubble with great, silver paddles cutting through the air as they whirled in maddening circles. The strange object was descending. It was coming toward him. Around him, the other figures had stopped moving. They looked skyward but one could not tell from their faces if fear or relief lay beneath the ash and soot that covered them. Out of some primitive instinct to supplicant the gods, they, Matt included, gazed at the aberration a weary congregation of old and young seeking salvation.

Matt wondered if these were the emissaries of this strange planet in the bubbles or indeed gods, or perhaps they were one in the same. Around him a cloud of ash, and dust, and reddish stuff was kicked up by the landing craft obscuring all. Finally, the strange object landed and the whirling paddles stopped their incessant revolutions. Slowly, the cloud dissipated.

He watched with dispassion as three creatures in stark, white clothes jumped out of the bubble and came running toward him and the others. God, he thought, they must have showers here. Look how clean they are. I wonder if they will let me take a shower.

A moment later they reached him.

Chapter 25

HOME

EARLY SEPTEMBER 1966 – SAN FRANCISCO

Matt Samuels' parents and his sister met him at the Greyhound Bus station. They exchanged hugs and kisses, embraces all around. He carried with him his duffel bag over his shoulder and lots of memories. Clean-shaven now and with a bronzed tan, he was their son again, tall, lean, and home safely.

"Honey, I'm so glad you're home," his mother said joyfully and through moist eyes.

"Hey, big brother, it's good to see you," Rachel said with a wink.

"Welcome home, son," his father said evenly. "Welcome home."

Once back at the Diamond Heights house, Matt unpacked and then joined the family in the living room. They were listening to the latest war news from Vietnam. Apparently, things were not going well. His dad quickly turned off the television. They wanted to know everything about the fire and his escape. Well mainly his mother and Rachel. His father seemed unusually quiet even for him.

He told them about being in the hospital for a few days to take care of a few dozen assorted cuts, scratches, minor burns, and, most importantly, to square away his head. The same was true for the other fellows. As for Doug, he was getting better. Frank's concussion was short-lived owing to his hard-hat, or harder head. And the old guy, Larry, well he pulled through with a high dose of vitamins and lots of rest and good food. All the summer workers would soon return to their homes. Frank and Doug as fulltime CDF employees would man the home front during the fall and winter months with a skeleton crew.

And he told them about the three firefighters from San Diego, who hadn't listened to him and died when the fire caught up to them on a road to nowhere.

He told them about the rescue making it seem easier than it was at the time. He didn't tell them how close it had been. They were amazed to hear the story of the water drop and the borate bomber.

The fire, he told them, burned all around them and through the woods. It didn't get to Portland but only the rain stopped it in southern Oregon. The people who knew something about fires called it one of the worst in California history. For those who fought it, the Happy Camp Fire will always be "the fire." And the guys he worked with would always be his friends who spent one hell of a day together in August 1966.

When he was finished, his mother asked him if he would return to the CDF next summer. He said he would.

"Matt, is that really necessary?" she asked. "Dad can fix you up with another job."

"But I like this job, mom."

"You like this job. How can you say that? You almost got killed."

"I'm considering going into the CDF after college."

"What?" she almost screamed. "What are you talking about? You wanted to be a history major, didn't you? You wanted to teach."

"Mom, try to understand. I have a feeling for fire. I want to be part of a team that stops it from hurting people. I'm thinking about enrolling at Humboldt State College."

"I don't understand."

"It's like being a policeman. I want to protect people. The only difference is I don't go after murderers and good old-fashioned American mobsters. I fight another kind of enemy. They have a great Forestry program at Arcata."

"Matt's got a point, mom.," Rachel said. He should do what he wants."

"Rachel!"

"Mom, let' talk about something else."

"Matt, I just want you to be safe. That's all I want. Please think about it."

"I will."

Matt went up to his room and sat down on his bed. Wow, it was nice to be back in his old room and to have a clean, soft bed to sleep in tonight. He thought about what he had been through. Waking up in the hospital had really shaken him. For a moment he questioned his own sanity. The shrink explained he had been through a terribly traumatic experience --- that he was OK. He just needed a little rest. He felt better when he heard the other guys were fine, but dealing with the same trauma as he.

On the ride back to San Francisco, he thought about his summer. He had to admit, it was the best time of his life. He knew, if he could, he would return next summer. He would challenge the red menace again. And, if necessary, he would taste the wind once more.

His mind shifted to school. He wasn't quite ready for academia, but he would enroll at Humboldt. He would sit through lectures, take notes, write papers, and take the required tests. How totally boring all of that seemed compared to what he had been through. But he needed a degree and somewhere in the future he would work for the CDF.

He heard a noise. He looked up and was surprised to see his father standing in the doorway.

"Dad."

"Matt."

"Good to be back."

"Good to have you back, son."
"Something on your mind, Dad?"
"Go easy on your mom. She was really scared."
"Gotcha."
"One other thing, Matt…"
"Yes."

Matt's father didn't answer him directly. He walked over and hugged his son, and then pulled out the letter he had stashed away days before.

"Matt, I didn't show this letter to your mother. Rachel doesn't know about it either. It's addressed to you. You decide what you want to do, and then tell them when you're ready."
"Sure, dad."

Robert Samuels gave his son the letter face down and walked out of the room leaving his son alone. Matt looked at the envelope's backside. It indicated nothing. He turned it over and read the return address --- *Selective Service Administration, Washington D.C.*

Matt Samuels was back home and he "could taste the wind."

APPENDIX

In 1934 the government collected stories from the C.C.C. and published them in a book entitled *Youth Rebuilds.* As already noted, my father's story, *Forest Fire,* was included and inspired me to write *Taste the Wind.*

Chronology can be a human timeline. My father was 18 in 1915 when he joined the U.S. Navy. He was 22 when his tour of duty was up in 1919. He was 32 when the Great Depression began in 1929, and almost 36 when he joined the C.C.C. in 1933. He was nearly 39 when he left the C.C.C. in late 1935. Within a few weeks after Pearl Harbor in December 1941, he was called back into the Navy. He was 45-years old. He would be discharged from the Navy in 1946 age of 49.

FOREST FIRE BY SAMUEL LIVINGSTON

"FIRE! FIRE! Every man out to fight forest fire!"

Orders fly thick and fast. "Take two blankets, nothing more, and pile into the open truck! Sit on the floor, or stand up, which ever is most comfortable. But get going!"

It is the afternoon of July 5, 1933. A blazing sun is overhead. "All ready?" shouts the ranger-chauffeur. "Lt's go!"

He takes the steering wheel in his massive hands and the 1916th Company, Civilian Conservation Corps, made up of World War veterans, and stationed at Arroyo Grande, California, moves up for its first battle with the Red Menace. There is excitement aplenty.

The ranger swings the truck around a fast turn and catapults down around the rim of a canyon. Then up, around, and down again. A few minutes of this and we are dizzy. We lose all sense of direction. Only the hot ball of sun gives us any idea of our general way.

These pretzel-like roads are built for emergencies such as we are now facing. They are so winding and twisting that we cross the dry headwaters of the Salinas River seventeen times in nineteen miles

It is more refreshing now. The sun is out of our path and a breeze has sprung up. A soft, red-brown sky clings to the horizon. A stretch of green sycamores is balm to our dust-filled eyes. The monotonous brush gives way to green pastures. We stop for a moment to place our parched lips to canteens of water.

"Where's the fire?" we ask the ranger.

"Just around the corner," he replies with a sly grin. He knows that we are green.

Towns glide by. People dine leisurely in fine restaurants and we gaze on like vultures. We try to snatch a bit of rest, but it's no use. There is no relief from this swaying, crowded monster. A dark, foreboding mountain looms ahead and we tremble at the thought of the coming ascent.

At last, past the midnight hour, we grind to a stop before a ranger outpost. There are a few hasty words. "She's roaring." The outpost tells Bill, our driver. He shoots the truck ahead.

From there on it is an endurance test to see how long our nerves will stand up under continuous hammer. Morning comes with ill-humor at a high level. We cloak ourselves in blankets and look like wild Arabs.

At noon the truck comes to an abrupt stop in a clearing. We rub our sleepy eyes and tumble out. Steaming beans, stew and coffee are put before us. But we lay our worn bodies on the ground.

Hardly have we stretched our bones when we are aroused by the Camp Boss's cry, "All hands up!" There is nothing else to do but obey. I the distance a spout of red flame stretches to the sky; white some hangs over the horizon. We breakfast hurriedly and pester the ranger in charge with questions. "You are at China Camp, base depot." We are told. "The fire is burning on Black Cone Mountain, in the Monterey Division of the Santa Barbara National Forest."

Food and an hour's sleep restore our strength and we snap into it again. All hands are mustered and counted off. An eight pound brush ax, lumberman's ax, or a shovel is issued each of us besides a gallon canteen of water and a bag of sandwiches. We make a knapsack of our blankets, sling it across our shoulder, and await the word to move up.

Pack trains are loading with foodstuffs and supplies. A seating muleteer, bullwhip in hand, puffs away at a strong pipe. Trucks stand by and we wonder if we have to ride in them again. No! The only way to get to our destination, Pine Ridge Camp, is by hiking.

"Move up!" comes from the Camp Boss, and with a wiry ranger at our head we start on our way. In the cool of the early morning we ache unmercifully. Before we have gone a mile, however, our feet and legs commence to ache and we shift our pack from one shoulder to the other.

Between China Camp and Pine Ridge Camp there is a difference in altitude of over two thousand feet. More than that, the way is over the most dangerous, twisting, and entirely exposed-to-sun that man or beast ever trod. It led for the most through dense brush. At places many a man almost lost his footing on loose rock or false gravel.

Shortly after noon every drop of water in our canteens is emptied and w are strung over a line a mile long. Lunches are thrown away to lighten burdens, feet are swollen, and blistered, legs are tired and we crumple down many times to rest. The heat is intense, almost unbearable.

We are too troubled to enjoy the great hush, the beauty and majesty of the wilderness. Later, on our return from the fire, we lingered along the trail and nature's magnificence and glory rewarded us many fold.

Then suddenly there is a jubilant shout. "There's the camp! Down there!" We look down upon a clearing in a stand of pines. Men are moving about. In some mysterious way, we take full strides and with a show of bravado begin the descent.

"When do we eat?" we shout as we enter the camp.
"Right now," retorts the Camp Boss, "Line up and get it!"

Pine Ridge Camp, we learn, is one of the fire camps scattered throughout the forest. It is the nearest point from which men and stores can be assembled to fight the fire. The country is almost impenetrable, rough and covered with a dense growth of chaparral, manzanita, and other brush. The only means of fighting the fire, we are told, is to try and confine it to a limited area.

The heavens to the south are aflame. Flashes of fire shoot out of the depths of the canyon. Billows of white smoke sweep in a wide circle. A low roar, like far off thunder, falls on our ears.

Shortly after our meal the Camp Boss approaches us. "I want twenty-five men," he says, "for a dangerous job." Every man volunteers... He counts off the first twenty-five. A ranger takes charge and they march away. It will be a week before we meet again. The rest of us get some sleep.

We breakfast under the stars before dawn. Then we shoulder tools and canteens and hit the trail south. The flames loom up in the darkness like fiery volcanoes. We move along silently between walls of brush until the fire appears to be about two miles away. We can go no further. The ranger sizes the situation quickly.

"We'll make a firebreak here," he says. "That should hold her."

After instructions are given, we squeeze in, our axes striking against the tough bark of manzanita and chaparral. So eager are we to make good that before the brush falls to the ground it is picked and dragged away. The trail is widened and cleared to eighteen feet. That's where the term "firebreak" comes in. It means exactly what it says--- break the fire. The lack of fuel is supposed to stop the spread of the flames.

At the base of the brush, there is a thick mat of inflammable matter---decayed leaves, moss and soil --- the deposit of years, interwoven, twined and twisted with the roots of trees and brush. This must be removed, otherwise the work we have already done is in vain. It is a mean job. In places it is necessary to go down on our knees and pick it apart with our hands.

There is no time for rest. The hard, exhausting labor under the broiling sun saps our strength. It seems as though the very blood is being sucked ourt of our veins. Water is scarce. The fiery monster also brings to its aid bugs, insects, deer flies and gnats which light savagely on our faces. Scorpions with lobster-like claws keep us on the jump. There are rattlesnakes. You cannot escape itching or poison oak very long. The brush is thick with stinging nettles and wood ticks.

By late afternoon the firebreak is extended up-grade, along a mile front. We are suddenly faced with a towering mass of rock, and from its pinnacle have an excellent view of the fire. It is eating its way out of its narrow confines, sweeping along in a circle and roaring with he thunder and frightfulness of a hurricane. Still, for some unknown reason, everything seems calm. We stand in awe, more like puppets than human beings. The sky is deep crimson and a wall of smoke seems to be holding it aloft. Deer and smaller animals flee before the flames. Some my have fallen or may have been trapped in their flight, for buzzards hover overhead. The sun cuts short our reverie and we crawl down the jagged rocks like goats, cutting away brush and trees to the dry creek below. Misery is born and reborn. We cry for water and rest.

"Let the fire burn! Let the whole damn forest burn!" we murmur in agony. The ugly flames race along and we remember our solemn oath --- to carry out all orders. We drive ourselves on. But flesh and blood can stand only so much. Darkness falls mercifully and we are ordered in. A plane wings over our heads, making a survey. A rumor starts down the line that reinforcements are coming.

Approaching camp we hera many voices and we straighten our shoulders. Yes, reinforcements! One hundred and fifty at least, husky Civilian Conservation Corps boys from camps in Santa Barbara, Monterey and San Luis Obispo counties, who joined up in Ohio and Indiana. They give us big hand and we return the compliment.

At two o'clock the following morning we hit the trail together. Side by side we work. These youngsters go to it like demons. They laugh and sing as though they are on a picnic, and we are imbued with their gay spirit. A fine bond of comradeship develops between us --- we veterans, and they, youngsters who were only babes on their mothers' knees when we answered the call in 1917.

The fire eats its way slowly out of the canyon towards the firebreaks, as expected, then appears o die down. We comfort ourselves with the thought that morning will see it under control. Half of the men are permitted to return to camp. Some continue clearing the flammable materials. Others are posted to watch. The rest take a nap.

"Here she comes! Here she comes!" Two men on lookout come tearing down, destroying the calm of the early morning with their terrifying cries.

The conflagration is coming toward us through a steep banked canyon, burning up everything in its path. Rocks are loosened and tumble down the banks. Burning brands and crisp cones are hurled through the air.

"Back fire!" comes the order along the line. We hardly hear it, but every man of us somehow seems to know what to do. Standing on the fire side of the break, we pour oil on the brush and set fire to it.

A friendly breeze throws it back on the oncoming fire.

A stand of stately redwood looks down upon us with dignity. But not for long... The flames eat up the long trunks, consuming the bark, foliage and branches. The noise sounds like the "puff, puff" of a thousand locomotives. Clumps of pine, highly resinous, take fire instantly.

A crew hacking a break along a hog back, with their backs to a rocky wall, are suddenly cornered by a red tongue. "Look out!" we want to scream, but the cry chokes in our throats. The men pale momentarily, then with desperate energy clear a space and drop to the ground on their bellies. Miraculously, the flames sweep over their heads and sift to one side. They go right on with their work. Another group scales the most perpendicular wall of a jutting canyon and stamps out a blaze.

The battle goes on along a zig-zag front. We fight from the crests, brows, sides and bottoms. The youngsters were real heroes. No army going over the top ever fought with greater zeal, courage, and willingness. Reckless and impetuous to a fault, they would have rushed right into the very mouth of the inferno if not held back.

Night, with its damp atmosphere, comes to our aid and we gain the upper hand. A mounted ranger tells us that reinforcements are battling the flames au five miles south along the North Fork of the Sur River. These intrepid men, after building a line of firebreaks around Tassajara Hot Springs, a resort southwest of Black Cone, and stopping the flames which endangered it, crossed over Tony's Trail with forty=pound packs on their backs. They continued in the darkness of night right through boulder-filled Willow Creek, between walls rising three hundred feet. No pack train dared make the ascent. They built an emergency camp and before they had opportunity to rest received orders to march to our aid. And at early dawn they came in. Among this mixed group of veterans and youngsters are our twenty-five comrades who left us days back.

A thousand men battle along the line. After three more days and nights of relentless warfare the fire is pushed back. The flames, though subdued, are not fully conquered. Reinforcements come up and take our place on the line.

They patrol the burned area to prevent any new outbreaks. And this they did until July 21, when the fire was officially reported under control. It burned about 7,000 acres, endangering at all times the water supply, if not actually the towns of such well known places as Santa Barbara, San Luis Obispo and Carmel.

We wish them a short stay and with a wave of the hand bid them "happy days." Tonight we sleep the sleep of peace. The earth is as soft as down. The coolness of Pine Ridge Camp lulls us. We stretch our hands like babes to pluck a star and fall asleep clutching tightly to the heavenly jewel.

Samuel Livingston
Company 1916, CCC
Arroyo Grande, California

Printed in the United States
by Baker & Taylor Publisher Services